A Haras of Horses

A Joy Forest Cozy Mystery

Blythe Ayne

A Haras of Horses

A Joy Forest Cozy Mystery

Blythe Ayne

A Haras of Horses
A Joy Forest Cozy Mystery
Blythe Ayne

Emerson & Tilman, Publishers
129 Pendleton Way #55
Washougal, WA 98671

www.BlytheAyne.com
Blythe@BlytheAyne.com

A Haras of Horses
ebook ISBN: 978-1-957272-00-9
Paperback ISBN: 978-1-957272-01-6
Large Print ISBN: 978-1-957272-02-3
Hardbound ISBN: 978-1-957272-03-0
Audio ISBN: 978-1-957272-04-7

[**FICTION** / Mystery & Detective / Cozy / General
FICTION / Mystery & Detective / Women Sleuths
FICTION / Mystery & Detective / Cozy / Cats & Dogs]

BIC: FM

DEDICATION

*Welcome to all who love horses
and mystery.*

Table of Contents

A few words about the place, the time....

Dr. Joy Forest, a social scientist, is called to her childhood home for an emergency, but then discovers a mystery ... what happened to the neighbor's gorgeous black stallion that suddenly disappeared?

The year is 2032. Although the times are somewhat different, people are ever the same—lovable or loathsome, truthful or deceitful, generous or selfish, courageous or timid, loyal or treacherous, *but always a mystery!*

This is Joy's world. It's not much different from yours. Come now to the Great Northwest and discover with Joy what has happened to the beautiful horse, as well as what all the swirling, whirling, unfolding events reveal to her heart....

Chapter 1

A Horse Named Grifter

"Y ou had better do something about that horse of yours!" Aunt Claudia squawked when I reluctantly connected with her call, tearing me from my concentration on my Kashmir project.

"Hold," I commanded the nuralnet, feeling anxious. The beautiful translucent colors of the 3-D that surrounded me shrank to a bubble. I swiveled my chair around, turning my back on my work, concerned about my beloved horse.

"Are you talking about Grifter?"

"Do you have another horse?"

"No, Aunt Claudia. Grifter is my only much-adored-but-expensive horse. Is he all right?" I rarely had time to be with Grifter, but I adored him, and I didn't want any bad news.

"Well, the bad news is…."

Dang! I just told fate not to give me any bad news.

Aunt Claudia rattled on, "He's whining. Whining and whining. It's driving me nuts."

"Whining?" What did she mean by that? "Do you mean 'whinnying'?"

"No, Joy. I do not mean whinnying. I know what I'm saying, please do not patronize me."

"No. No patronizing, Aunt Claudia. It's just, you know, people don't usually refer to any sound that a horse makes as 'whining.'"

"He's *whining*," Aunt Claudia insisted. "He sounds like a … I don't know … he sounds like a child, or a dog. *Whine! Whine! Whine!* That's all he does."

I stood up and paced up and back, up and back. Robbie, the robo cat joined me, pacing up and back alongside me. I couldn't quite imagine Grifter whining. He wasn't a brave horse, but he seldom complained about anything. "Is he eating?"

"Yes," Aunt Claudia said. Then she giggled, a sound I'd rarely heard from her. "He's eating like a horse."

"Oh, yeah, eating like a horse, ha ha, funny. So, that's good. Is he whining right now?"

"Probably."

"You can't hear him?"

"He's out in the pasture, along the fence, his head hanging over into the neighbor's field."

I wondered how that was relevant, but so concerned about Grifter "whining"—whatever that meant—that I didn't go into it. "Is he not well?"

"There doesn't seem to be anything wrong with him," Aunt Claudia said, becoming yet more testy.

"What does Uncle Eben say about Grifter whining?"

"Well, I don't know."

"You haven't asked him?" This seemed improbable, as Aunt Claudia was *always* bending Uncle Eben's ear with one complaint or another.

"No, I didn't ask him. I've been *telling* him. Grifter's whining is making me lose my mind."

"Is Uncle Eben there?"

"He's in town, getting groceries." I could sense Aunt Claudia tapping her foot with my, I'm sure she thought, extreme obtuseness.

I looked over my shoulder at the little 3-D bubble of my project hovering above my desk, its deadline fading away. "Has the vet looked at Grifter?"

"Yes, your uncle had Charley come out. They stood in the pasture with Grifter and shot the breeze for *two hours*. When they came back in, Charley said there wasn't anything physically wrong with the horse. He thinks Grifter is lonely. Since we got rid of the three sheep, he's the only creature on the property, except for the field mice and raccoons."

"If he's just lonely, the only thing I could do is buy another horse to keep him company." Dollar signs floated off in my mind's eye.

"Oh heavens, Joy, *do not* get another horse! One is too many."

I refused to agree with her, although she was frustratingly correct.

"I can't come right now. I'm in the middle of a huge...."

"I know, Joy, you're in the middle of a huge project. You're always in the middle of a huge project. But really, if you don't do something about this horse noise, I'll have to do something."

Was she threatening me? I felt my brow furrow. "What does that mean?"

"I might have to put him up for sale."

Now I began to get angry. One of my life lessons is to learn how to not let Aunt Claudia get under my skin. Like she was doing now. "No, you won't, Aunt Claudia," I said with quiet reserve. "He's my horse, I have the papers to prove it, and you will not sell my horse. Anyway, Uncle Eben wouldn't let you."

Although I was pushing her about as far as I've ever pushed, I knew I had her there. Uncle Eben would never allow Grifter to be sold out from under me, even if I didn't have the horse's ownership papers in my safe. Which I do. *So, take that, dear Auntie!*

I sighed in resignation. "I'll come out tomorrow morning, Aunt Claudia. But if I'm going to do that, I've really got to get to work. I'll see you in the morning. Much love to you and Uncle Eben. Bye now." I hung up without waiting for a response.

* *

"P*leeeaze* let me come with you, Joy. I want to meet Grifter," Robbie nagged me the next morning, standing on his hind legs, his front paws together prayerfully.

"No, Robbie," I muttered in distraction, tearing around my bedroom, trying to think of everything I needed to take with me. Knowing I'd probably leave the most important thing behind.

"But ...."

"Robbie, please. I must think." I stood looking into my backpack. What wasI forgetting?

"AR glasses," Robbie said.

"Right." I grabbed up my augmented reality glasses and put them in the backpack. I threw my hands up. "That'll have to do. I've gotta get on the road."

I picked up the backpack and turned. *Arg!* I couldn't ignore Robbie's expression. "Don't try to work me, Robbie, dear. If it was just you, it wouldn't be much of a problem. But packing up Dickens, and worrying about him there...."

"I'll take care of Dickens!"

"Yes, you will. Right here, thank you kindly. I'll take you to meet Grifter some other time, when ... when...."

"When Grifter isn't whining?"

"Yes. When Grifter isn't whining." I reached over to pet Dickens-the-bio-cat, in his usual spot, curled up asleep on the bed, then stooped to pet Robbie. "I'm counting on you, you know. I'm running off half-cocked, and I need you to be my eyes and ears here at the home front. Okay, I *must go*."

Robbie followed me to the back door while I ordered my self-driving car to come into the drive, but he stopped begging me to come along, which was a relief.

"Okay my furry friend, I'm off."

"When will you be back?"

"*Oh!*" The thought had not yet crossed my mind. "I … I don't know. In a couple days, I hope. You'll be the first to know." I stepped out the back door, threw my backpack onto the backseat of the car, and climbed in the front. "Uncle Eben's," I ordered.

"Road trip!" the car exclaimed. "It's been a while."

"Yes, it has." I didn't feel like idle chat at the moment. I needed to dictate into my wrist comp a few points I must not forget about to my disrupted Kashmir project. And I needed to get ready to be with Aunt Claudia—not the easiest experience. But most importantly, I needed to think about Grifter. What could possibly be wrong with him?

It was only a two-hour drive to my childhood home outside of Leavenworth, Washington, not nearly enough time to do all the thinking I needed to think.

Suddenly, Aunt Claudia's raucous phone ring jolted me out of my dark reverie.

Chapter 2
The Old Home Place

I answered her call as I pulled into the driveway. "What's up, Aunt Claudia?"

"Where *are* you?" she demanded.

"In the driveway! What's the urgency?"

Without answering, she disconnected.

I got out of the car and reached in the back for my backpack. As I did so, I heard a horrible grinding sound, like some machinery about to quit working.

I stepped inside the little mid-twentieth century farmhouse—like stepping back in time to visit my childhood home. I was ready to give my aunt and uncle their hugs, but I could see Aunt Claudia, her body tense, her brow furrowed, was not in a hug-receiving mood. She stood in the kitchen, her usual neatly pressed self, wearing one of her flower print cotton house dresses, covered by a spanking clean apron, her shoulder-length, graying hair severely tied back.

"Where's Uncle Eben?"

"In the pasture, with your horse."

"Oh dear! Is he really sick?"

"Why would you ask that?" she asked in a testy voice. "There's nothing wrong with your uncle."

"I'm not asking if Uncle Eben is sick! And why would he be in the pasture if he was? I'm asking if Grifter is sick."

Things have reached a new level of wacky around here, I thought.

"Well, Joy, we don't know. Now that you're here, he had better calm down. And I mean your horse, not your uncle!"

I guffawed out loud. "Oh, Aunt Claudia, you made a joke!" I went up to her and forced a hug on her, whether she liked it or not. That unearthly machine sound seemed to augment as we stood there in an awkward hug that my aunt refused to return.

"What is this weird sound, Aunt Claudia? It's like some machinery is falling apart."

"That weird sound, Morning Joy, is *your horse!*"

Wow! We were in unchartered territory for my aunt to call me by my birth name, which was rarely mentioned. "That sound is Grifter?! How is it *possible?*"

I didn't even bother to go to my tiny childhood bedroom to throw down my backpack. I flung it on the sofa and hurried out the back door. "We'll get to the bottom of this, Auntie, don't worry," I said, worrying enough for both of us. I'd never heard such a sound from any creature in my life!

There stood Grifter in the pasture, head hanging over the fence, making an impossibly huge and piteous sound. I hurried up to him and Uncle Eben, who was patting him and making soothing sounds that had no effect on Grifter, whatsoever.

Uncle Eben, on the far side of Grifter, didn't see me approach. "*What* is going on with my horse?" I asked in the lull between two bouts of Grifter's weird noise.

"*Oh! Joy!* You startled me," Uncle Eben looked at me around Grifter's neck. "We have no idea what's wrong with him. He makes this, how would you describe it? *Sound*, pretty much all day, and into the night. Sometimes even in his sleep! The vet says it's the weirdest thing he's ever encountered."

"Yeah. Weird." I tried to pull Grifter's head from hanging over the fence, but he wouldn't let me. It cut me to the quick that he didn't even acknowledge me. "But Uncle Eben, there's something seriously wrong with him! He won't even look at me. How is it possible Charley didn't find anything?"

"I don't know, Joy. I really don't know. I agree with you, there *must* be something wrong with him. But if the doctor can't find anything, what are we to do?"

This was a new sort of mystery. I stood there petting my sad, depressed horse, wondering what could possibly cause him to make this noise. One of the many things I loved about Grifter, even though he's not the most beautiful horse in the world, is that without fail, until this moment, he's always been happy to see me, and practically able to read my mind. Or, more accurately, my heart.

Being raised by Aunt Claudia had not been the easiest childhood. But Grifter, in my life since I was eleven, had soothed my pain. Yes, Uncle Eben was there. And after any of Aunt Claudia's many tirades at me, he'd come out to the barn to give me affection and support. But ... he still always defended Aunt Claudia's indefensible behavior.

Only Grifter gave me unconditional affection. Only Grifter seemed to understood how my heart hurt. Now it was *my* turn to take care of *him*. This terrible sound was grief, and if my presence didn't calm him, something other than my absence was the cause.

Like I say, a new mystery.

"I could hear him crying from the driveway, Uncle Eben! I thought a piece of machinery was breaking down. No wonder Aunt Claudia is at her wit's end." I had to practically shout to be heard above Grifter.

Uncle Eben came around Grifter and stood beside me. "Let's go to the barn where can hear ourselves."

I nodded, reluctant to leave Grifter, now that I was here. We walked uphill to the cool, shadowy barn, and found a couple of bales of straw to sit on.

"If Charley is convinced that Grifter is not dealing with some physical malady, yet he's showing such profound distress, and *more to the point*, not even acknowledging me, there's *something* causing his grief."

Uncle Eben picked up a stick and poked it around in the straw at his feet. We both studied his moves as if the answers to our questions would magically appear in the straw, like tea leaves in the bottom of a cup. "I think you're right, Joy." He paused. "I think you're right. Though it seems too huge a reaction for...."

I held my breath, waiting for him to tell me what Grifter's huge reaction might be attributed to. Finally, losing my patience, I asked, "For what, Uncle Eben, for *what?*"

"Well…" He maddeningly paused again, then finally continued. "Grifter formed a bond with a horse that lived next door. I noticed he spent most of where he is right now, with his head over the fence, looking into the neighbor's pasture." Uncle Eben glanced up at me and then back down at his handiwork, stirring up the straw. Did he feel guilty?

Strange. I kept my silence.

"I hate to admit this, but I really haven't paid much attention to Grifter of late. He appeared content. But when that stallion next-door disappeared…."

"*Disappeared!*" I exclaimed, shocked. "What do you mean, the stallion next door disappeared?"

"Just that. The guy next door bought that gorgeous black Arabian stud, did you happen to see him?"

I nodded. I'd noticed the beautiful horse the last couple of times I'd been to my childhood home. But I had no idea Grifter had formed an attachment to him.

"Strangely enough, that black stallion befriended Grifter in return," Uncle Eben continued. "Especially strange, given that he had three beautiful mares to keep him company. Anyway, a few days ago, that black stallion disappeared. Then I heard through the rumor mill that he'd been stolen."

"That's terrible! The neighbor must be distraught. What does he say?" I'd never met the current neighbor, who had moved in only a couple years previous.

"Well, Joy, I know this probably seems a little weird, but I've not talked to him. Ahm ... that's not quite accurate. I tried a couple times, but he was not open to conversation. In fact, he was quite *rude*. If you think your Aunt Claudia can be difficult, she's a Sunday school picnic compared to that guy."

Unbelievable! Everyone adores my Uncle Eben. He's the sweetest, most easy-going person on the planet. And he almost never said anything bad about anyone, no matter how much they deserved it. His negative comment about the neighbor was un-precedented.

"Are you sure he didn't sell the horse, or move him somewhere else?"

"No. Both Charley and Myles told me the horse has been stolen. It's a pretty big deal, because, I guess, that stud is famous in horse circles. And you know, we have our horse circles here."

Oh yes, it's a horsey community, I knew.

But … a horse thief! That was unacceptable. That was a horse of an entirely different color.

At that moment, I heard Grifter screaming at yet a new level of distress. I jumped up and ran out into the pasture.

Chapter 3

Grifter's Grief

As I flew out of the barn and into the pasture, I saw Grifter flinging his head about wildly, making the terrible, piteous sound.

I ran up to him, and, endangering myself, tried to grab onto his mane. I looked over my shoulder to see Uncle Eben running after me. "Get the halter!" I yelled.

Uncle Eben turned on his heels and ran back into the barn, soon returning with a halter and lead.

"Hey, hey, Grifter, it's all right. It's all right, my friend."

Uncle Eben came up quietly and handed me the halter, as Grifter calmed down a bit. I slipped the halter over his head, continuing to pat him and talk softly. "I think he realized I was here, and then I was gone, and he freaked out. I'm here, don't worry, my friend."

Grifter leaned his head into my shoulder, his breath calming. "See? Everything is going to be all right. It's going to be all right."

I started to walk him around the pasture, and he followed me like a docile little lamb. "That's it, we'll go for a walk, and you can tell me what's bothering you." I continued to chatter softly as Grifter padded alongside me—I didn't even need the lead.

Uncle Eben stood by the fence, a troubled grin on his face. I knew how to read his expression. Yes, a great relief to see that Grifter could be calmed. But also, a great problem. Uncle Eben knew I couldn't stay here permanently, just to keep Grifter happy.

One problem at a time, I thought. I felt reassured that Grifter, now behaving like his usual self, didn't have something physically wrong with him. I checked that concern off the list.

But it left the burning question: was he really that distraught over a missing neighboring horse? And the much bigger burning question: *Who stole the horse?!?*

We made a couple of circuits around the pasture, then I took Grifter into the barn. I settled down on the bale of straw I'd been sitting on earlier, and Grifter stood as close to me as he could. I patted his muzzle. Uncle Eben followed us into the barn and sat back down on his bale of straw.

"Well, that's something," he said, looking at Grifter, shaking his head. "You're the Grifter whisperer, Joy."

I chuckled softly. "I hope so! After all, we've been best pals for years." I looked up at Grifter, "Haven't we?"

Grifter neighed quietly.

"But—what do we do now?" Uncle Eben asked pragmatically. "*What* do we do now?"

"A couple of things come to mind. One, try to get to the bottom of the horse theft and see if we can't find the missing horse, or two, the obvious option of getting Grifter a companion. He needs another creature in his life. And he deserves it."

Uncle Eben didn't say anything, but he nodded in reluctant agreement.

"Aunt Claudia said you got rid of the three sheep, which is a pity."

"I liked the sheep. I liked seeing the beauty of them in the pasture. But your aunt said they were an unnecessary expense," Uncle Eben's voice was sad. "They really didn't cost much. We had them since they were little lambs, given to us by the Melichar boy who decided he didn't want to complete his 4-H project. I didn't know we'd end up keeping them. But, as I say, I quite liked them.

"Your aunt said they were too much work for me. But really, I enjoyed attending to them, feeding them, chatting with them...."

"Oh! Uncle Eben, I've it breaks my heart to hear this. I didn't know you were that attached to the sheep. I forgot the story about how you came to have them. But if you loved them...."

"Well, love is a bit strong."

"Is it? Really? You just expressed love for those three beautiful little sheep."

"*Hmmm*, okay, I guess I did love them. I didn't realize how much I'd miss them—until they were gone."

"So, you're missing the sheep, and Grifter is missing the sheep. I wonder if you can get the sheep back?"

"They got split up. I gave them away with the stipulation that they were *pets,* and were to go to homes that would welcome them and treat them as pets. Some folks came and got two of them. They live a couple hours away, so I haven't seen them since they left. And the single one I gave to Lucy, in town. She has that great big yard, and the sheep grazes it so she doesn't have to mow. I think the little sheep is happy there. I drive by now and then, just to take a look at her." He sighed deeply. "Yeah, it's true, I do still miss them...."

"*Ohhh!*" I could say nothing more.

"But, of course, you aunt was right. They cost money for no return."

"Except the only return that's meaningful. *Love!*" I withheld voicing the rest of my thought—that love was not Aunt Claudia's strong point.

"Shall we go in?" Uncle Eben asked, standing. "I'll bet you haven't had any breakfast, being on the road since early morning."

"No, I haven't, but I don't need it. I'm concerned about leaving Grifter so soon after getting him settled. No point in getting him all riled up again. I think I'll stay out here for a while."

Uncle Eben nodded. "You make a good point. I'll bring you out a little something."

I watched him walk out of the barn, and for the first time in forever, I saw he was not the robust and agile man I knew in my childhood. He was aging. It tore me up. I knew this trip would be difficult—but I didn't know it would be in all the ways that were piling up.

*   *

Uncle Eben returned with some toast and tea and a basket of fruit—enough to last me three days!

"I'm not moving into the barn," I laughed, giving him a hug.

"Well, I couldn't recall your favorite fruit, so I brought something of everything we have in the kitchen."

"The strawberries look scrumptious!"

"Yep. I've grown great strawberries this year." He gave me a small wave as he went off to do a bunch of chores, and I settled in with my tea and toast and a plethora of fruits.

After my modest breakfast, while sitting on a bale of straw, Grifter hovering over me the whole time, I got up and led him into his stall. I found a couple of horse blankets and spread them out on the clean straw, then settled myself on the comfortable makeshift bed. I had a passing thought that I should get some work accomplished. I had my wrist comp —I could do some dictation and be constructive.

But on another hand, it felt so lovely to *do nothing*. Most unusual for me, if I was awake. Adding to the warm fuzzies, Grifter lay down in the straw next to me. Cozy as a couple of peas in a pod. Well, if one of the peas was *ginormous*.

But then a staggering exhaustion came over me. I tried to remember the last time I'd simply *stopped*. I couldn't remember such a time. I fell into a deep sleep, awakened hours later by a soft whinnying from Grifter. I sleepily looked around the stall and saw Aunt Claudia, standing in the doorway, holding a tray.

"You were sound asleep."

"I was! We both were." I patted Grifter.

"I brought you a sandwich."

"Brilliant! I'm *famished!*"

"Where do you want me to put the tray?"

"Right here on the blanket would be fine." I didn't quite know how to take her unfamiliar kindness.

She set the tray down on the blanket, then stepped back and folded her arms, appearing to feel as awkward as I did.

"Well …" we both said at the same moment. We chuckled.

"What were you going to say?" I asked, looking up at her.

"No, you, what were you going to say?"

"I … *I forget!*" I looked down at the tray where I beheld a beautiful avocado, lettuce, and tomato sandwich, piled high, looking delicious, along with a little teapot and teacup. "Oh! This is beautiful, Auntie. Thank you. Won't you join me?"

"I'll sit." She glanced around. "If I had something to sit on."

I jumped up and pulled the bale of straw outside of Grifter's stall around into the stall. "There. A bale of straw makes an acceptable chair, when necessary."

Cautiously, Aunt Claudia lowered herself onto the straw bale. "Oh," she said, sounding surprised, "that's fairly comfortable."

Had she lived on the farm her whole life, and *never* sat on a bale of straw? Hard to believe! I nodded, digging into the sandwich, gesturing to the other half. "Share this with me."

"No, Joy, I had my lunch. It looks as though you're hungry enough for the whole thing."

"I am," I said around a mouthful of avocado. "This is fabulous!"

Aunt Claudia nodded, but otherwise didn't acknowledge my compliment. I found myself wondering what else she had up her sleeve. And immediately felt guilty about the unkind thought.

"When are you coming in?" she asked.

"Ahm, I haven't thought about it. I'm all wrapped up in Grifter. And, look, he's so contented with me here."

"Yes. But, Joy, are going to move into the barn?"

"Hadn't planned on it."

"It's such a relief for him to be quiet," she said. "But … when you leave.…"

Now she was getting to her point. But—she had a valid point. "I know. There are problems. I'll take them on, one at a time. I'm pretty sure I understand why he's making that awful noise—Uncle Eben told me about the stolen stud.…"

"Oh, the 'stolen stud' story. I don't buy it!" she huffed.

"Really? What part do you not buy? That the stallion has been stolen, or that Grifter formed a strong bond with him?"

"That the horse was stolen."

Stymied, I asked, "You don't think he was stolen?"

"Who would steal something as big as a horse? And how would they do it without being seen?"

Wow! She was naïve.

"I believe a lot of people would attempt to steal a prized stud."

"What about his identity chip?"

Well now, she made a good point. As I hadn't had an identity chip implanted in Grifter, the thought had not yet crossed my mind. But a prized stud should have one. "I don't know! I'll ask Charley about that tomorrow. But, Auntie, people steal things much bigger than a horse all the time, and figure out ways of doing it.

"Anyway, what's important to me is that the horse is important to Grifter, and because of that, I want to see him back in his pasture."

"Yes. It would be good. But...." She trailed off.

"But what?"

"I think something's fishy."

"Oh!" This was news. "What do you mean? Isn't a horse being stolen fishy enough, or ... well, what do you mean?"

"I'm thinking that character next door is not moral, and I would say he did something with his own horse."

Yikes! Awful thought! "Like what, Aunt Claudia. Like what?"

"I don't know. I'm just saying, something is fishy."

"Like collecting insurance he may have taken out on the horse."

Aunt Claudia nodded. "Good thought, that."

Good thought, terrible result, if true. Because it would imply that he did away with his own gorgeous stallion, and thus, the horse would never come back to the neighboring pasture to make Grifter happy

I abandoned my sandwich. So many negatives. "I ... I hope you're wrong, Aunt Claudia."

"I hope so too." She stood. "Don't let it upset you too much. Eat your sandwich."

"I will." But I didn't feel like it. I took a sip of tea to show her I still had my appetite.

"Talk to you later. There's clean sheets on your bed."

"Oh!" I could not recognize my aunt! I don't think she had ever changed the sheets on my bed. Ever. Until today. "Thank you!"

She nodded and left the barn, while I sat on the horse blankets, processing the possibility of the neighbor having murdered his horse.

Very disturbing.

Grifter put his chin on my knee.

"You're my pal," I whispered, taking up the second half of my beautiful, delicious sandwich. After all, it had been made with a love that I never thought my aunt felt for me, and I would take in every crumb.

And then I fell back asleep.

I awoke with a start as a thunderous crack seemed intent on tearing the barn apart.

Chapter 4
Lightning and Thunder!

Whinnying, Grifter jumped up.

I jumped up too, groggy, confused, and, for a few moments, unable to figure out where I was.

Oh, right! In Uncle Eben's barn, with a gigantic thunderstorm roaring around the heavens—and roaring around the barn as well.

I reached out in the darkness to grab onto Grifter's ~~harness~~ HALTER lead. A bolt of lightning made the stall brighter than daylight. The whites of Grifter's eyes showed, and his whole body quivered. I feared he'd bolt from the barn as I finally managed to grasp his lead.

"It's all right, boy," I said softly. "Don't be scared, it's just a thunderstorm. We can use the rain!" I patted his neck, and he calmed down. "Let's go watch it." I lead him to the barn door.

We stood in the barn doorway, watching the fury of nature as it played out in the yard between the barn and the house. Lightning repeatedly brought everything into stark bas-relief between brilliant light and total darkness, accompanied by crashing thunder, the timpani of the gods. The sweet, pungent effervescence of ozone filled the air—invigorating!

I don't know when I enjoyed myself so much, as I stood there meditatively with my friend, Grifter. The ozone elevated my mood, and I considered running out into the storm to let the rain pummel me. But several practical thoughts ran through my mind in quick succession. One: I would then be all wet! Two: Grifter would join me and get all wet too, and three: and most importantly, *we could get struck by lightning!*

"And so, dear Grifter, I'm not going to go dancing in the rain! I'll stand here with you, enjoying it immensely in the shelter of the barn."

As we stood there, I saw the kitchen light come on. And then it immediately shut off. In the next lightning strike, I saw my uncle standing at the kitchen sink, looking out the window at the amazing nature show.

He saw Grifter and me in the barn doorway—we were kindred souls across the ocean of nature's display. I grinned. He smiled and waved, then returned his attention to the thunder, lightning, and rain. He'd stopped farming ten years previous, but he had a beautiful garden that would flourish from this rain.

The wild storm soon spent itself, and the next time I glanced at the house, no one stood at the kitchen window. Grifter and I made our way back to our cozy bed in his stall. I drank the now-cold tea— still delicious!—and reflected on all that I had to do during the day that just now crept an early morning light across the golden straw.

* *

"Now, Grifter, I'm going to go into the house, have a bit of breakfast, take a shower, and chat with my aunt and uncle. I need you to be calm while I do that." I took the lead off his halter. "Will you do that for me?"

He lowered his eyelids in contentment as I scratched between his ears. "Very good, stay like this, and we'll all be happy." I picked up the tray Aunt Claudia had brought out and went into the house.

Uncle Eben and Aunt Claudia were sitting at the little kitchen table, quietly sipping their morning beverage. I couldn't tell if I interrupted a conversation, or if they really were in a state of silent reverie. I put the tray on the counter and washed the plate, wiped the tray, then made myself a new pot of tea.

"Quite the storm last night!" I said, breaking the meditative silence.

"Exhilarating!" Uncle Eben agreed.

"I didn't even hear it," Aunt Claudia said. "I slept like a stone in a river, without Grifter making that horrible noise."

I laughed. "Goodness, Auntie, that storm must have been ten times louder than Grifter could ever possibly be!"

"It isn't the *volume*, it's the relentless grinding abuse of the *noise*." She got up and fussed around with re-washing the plate I'd just washed and re-wiping the tray, then putting them away. This was the aunt I knew! Nothing can be out of place for longer than a few moments, and only she knew how to clean things. "Tidy house, tidy mind!" she used to say to me when I was a child.

Which may be why my house is generally in disarray rather than "tidy." Since I got a lot of work done in my professional life, I suppose I felt I disproved her theory.

Or ... I was simply sort of a messy slug at heart.

I sat across the table from my uncle, and we shared a conspiratorial grin behind her back.

"Grifter and I stood in the doorway of the barn enjoying the spectacular show," I said.

Aunt Claudia turned and caught us. "What's that grin about?"

"Nothing!" I feigned innocence.

She shook her head and returned to the table. "What are your plans for the day?"

"Lots of thoughts, but not much plan. I want to talk to Charley about Grifter, of course. And pick his brain about the missing stud. Then I thought I'd talk with the neighbor."

They both made small gasps.

"I wouldn't advise it," Uncle Eben said.

"No. I wouldn't," Aunt Claudia agreed.

"Well, neither of you need to. But I do—maybe. I mean, I'm still thinking that part over. I'll see what Charley has to say. The neighbor isn't going to hurt me. He might be unpleasant, but he's not going to hurt me."

"He might hurt your feelings," Uncle Eben said.

"I don't know how. I don't know him, and I don't care what he says. I'm trying to get to the bottom of his missing horse. For my own interests, not his."

"He'll probably say something intolerable about your uncle," Aunt Claudia said. "You might feel you have to display some of your kung fu training."

"It's ju jitsu that I practice. With emphasis on 'practice,' rather than 'proficiency.' But, no. I'm not taking any bait he has to offer. I'm concerned about a horse, and that's all that matters. Two horses, that is. His stallion and my Grifter."

"I hope you listen to Charley if he advises against you talking with that awful person," Aunt Claudia said in a quiet voice, studying the interior of her mug.

Her concern for me touched and surprised me. Yet again! "I will, Aunt Claudia." And even if I would likely talk to the neighbor anyway, I wanted to reassure my aunt that I—*for sure!*—was not about to go onto someone else's property and start displaying my minimal martial arts talents.

"I think I'll start the day with a ride, and all the other bits will fall into place." I stood up to shower and change into my jeans.

"Aren't you going to have any breakfast?" Aunt Claudia asked.

I grabbed an apple from the fruit bowl. "This'll do."

I soon tore back through the kitchen on my way to the barn. "I'm off—don't look for me until you see the whites of my eyes."

"You're riding in those shoes?" Aunt Claudia asked, giving my footgear a disapproving look.

"They're fine. I'm only going for a casual ride, and I'm not going to see anyone."

"Your boots are in your closet."

Shock! She kept my boots?! "Really? You kept my boots from high school?"

"Of course. They were darn expensive, you know."

Yes. I knew. I'd saved up for them for half a year with the odd jobs I'd been able to come up with. Uncle Eben had promised to match my savings for the boots, dollar for dollar.

"Where have they been? I haven't seen them in years."

"Your uncle stumbled on them a few months ago in that big trunk you had in the barn and brought them in."

Although sorely tempted to go dig them out, I felt the day slipping away, and I wanted—urgently—to be on my favorite horse. "That is *so fantastic!* I'll dig them out later, but I gotta get on Grifter in what's left of this beautiful morning. Thank you for keeping them."

I hurried out the backdoor, thinking, *miracles abound!*

Full of that feeling for which I'd been named—Joy—I returned to the barn. Grifter, still in his stall, swung his head around and whinnied softly to me.

"What a great day, beautiful horse!" I started saddling him up, somewhat rusty as it had been a while. A couple of bridles still hung in the tack room, and I chose the dressy one. Grifter stood patiently as I fumbled getting the bit in his mouth and the bridle over his ears.

"Let's dress you up! I can't be bothered with putting my boots on, which I hope still fit, but you, dear Grifter, you get to dress up! It's been too long since we've gone for a good ride." I glanced out the barn door at the bright sunshine. "Look at this day! Bright and fresh after the rain." I brushed his mane and tail for a finishing touch, then climbed into the saddle.

It felt marvelous!

We came out of the barn and I hesitated, having not thought about where I intended to ride. I decided that simply going out on the road would be the easiest. There was almost no traffic on the little road, and everyone knew to drive cautiously in this horsey territory. I reined Grifter around my car, down the driveway, and out onto the road.

I wanted to talk with the neighbor who had the stolen stallion. But not right away. At this moment, I wanted to get back into the groove of a quiet ride. One of my favorite things in life was the meditative clip-clop of horse hooves against the road. I let Grifter amble along at his own preferred pace, leaving the reins lax in my hand. I even closed my eyes, basking in the warm sun, totally trusting Grifter to stay on the road.

I was entirely submerged in my own altered zone when I heard someone call out, "Is that you, Joy?"

Oh! My heart jumped at the sound of that voice, as much as I wished it would not.

Chapter 5
Meeting Myles

I opened my eyes and looked over my shoulder to see Myles coming up alongside me in his pasture beside the road, astride his gorgeous palomino, Amber.

"Yes. It's me. In the flesh. How're you doing, Myles?"

"I'm good. Better now. Jeez, you're a sight for sore eyes."

"Why are your eyes sore?"

"Funny, Joy. What brings you here? It's not a holiday."

"No, but it feels like one, being on Grifter." I swept out my hand, taking in the surroundings. "Could the day be more glorious?"

"No, Joy, it couldn't." He came up by me, and we ambled along side by side, with his property's fence between us.

"Amber is looking *spectacular!* How old is she now?"

"Pushing twenty, but in perfect health, thank goodness. She's such an excellent horse, and one of my best friends, if you know what I mean."

"I know exactly what you mean. It seems to slip my mind how much I love Grifter—until I see him, and then it all comes rushing back."

"Yeah. So, *ahm*, why, I ask again, are you here?"

"Can't I be here for no reason?"

"Yes. But not likely."

"You're right." Although it had been years since Myles and I had talked this much, he still knew me better than … perhaps better than I knew myself about some things. "I'm here because of the noise Grifter has been making. Aunt Claudia said she has, and I quote, 'nearly lost her mind' from his weird whining."

"Yeah, I've heard it. He's only been doing it for a few days, but it's quite penetrating. Carries on the wind."

"Oh dear! I'm lucky the neighbors haven't complained. Aunt Claudia threatened to sell Grifter even without neighbors complaining!"

"Oh!" Myles exclaimed, "she wouldn't dare!"

I was touched by his comment defending Grifter and me. "You're right, she really wouldn't dare. And couldn't carry it off in any case, as I have his ownership papers."

"And your uncle would not have it!"

"Right again, Myles. I even said as much to her, and she backed down. Anyway, it's good that Grifter is calmed by my presence."

"But … I assume you're not moving back here."

"You assume correctly."

"What are you going to do about Grifter if he needs you to be present in order not to make that horrific noise?"

We were now passing the neighbor's property. I gestured to his pasture. "Do you know this relatively new neighbor who has an extremely bad report from my aunt and uncle?"

"Not really. But I don't think much of him, either."

"It seems he had a horse that Grifter became bonded to. But, mysteriously, the horse has recently disappeared. Uncle Eben said Charley and you believe the horse was stolen."

"I did have that conversation with your uncle a couple days ago, but *my* information came from Charley, so there's really only one source."

"I see." I tried to keep my eyes on the road, but I couldn't help stealing a glance at Myles. He was a sight to behold. He rode beautifully, tall in the saddle with requisite cowboy hat, blue plaid shirt that matched his stunning sky-blue eyes, an endearing mop of sandy hair, jeans that looked like they were maybe a day old, but, knowing him, they were probably considerably older. And yes, boots. Of course.

Here he was, the man who broke my heart, although hardly more than a boy at the time. How is it he had become even more gorgeous?

He glanced over at me. "Nice boots," he observed with unmistakable sarcasm.

"Thanks," I answered, feigning innocence. "My aunt told me this morning that she saved my boots.…"

The ones you fell in love with in high school?"

"The very ones."

"Wow—that doesn't sound like her."

"I know!" I couldn't deny how great it felt to have someone know what I was talking about when I mentioned my aunt. "Shocking, yes. As I dashed to the barn to saddle up Grifter, she had a disparaging remark about my footgear—just like you. Then she knocked me for a loop by telling me Uncle Eben had come across my boots in a trunk in the barn where I'd kept some of my stuff, and she put them in the closet of my childhood bedroom.

"But, honestly, Myles, Grifter rides as well when I'm wearing casual shoes as when I'm wearing boots."

"Until he steps on you."

"He has never stepped on me!" I patted Grifter's neck. "And you never will, will you? Anyway, my concern is about this stallion that's been stolen that Grifter bonded with."

Myles shook his head. "It's a shame, whatever happened to that stud. He is—or was—a beautiful creature, who has produced some notable foal."

"Was? Oh dear, Aunt Claudia said something to the effect that she suspects the neighbor has done away with his own prized animal. It sounds like you share her suspicion."

"I don't know, Joy. But it's a possibility. One day the horse is there, the next day he's gone. Your neighbor didn't report him missing for an entire day. I only know this because I happened to ride by and I noticed the horse was missing. Because, yes, it's true, he often stood at the fence line, chatting with old Grifter here. Sort of an odd couple. But horses have their own way of establishing relationships."

"How does one dispose of a murdered horse?"

"Good question. But if someone stole the horse right from under your neighbor's nose, why did it take him a day to report it?"

"Another good question. And yet, if he's so awful and self-involved, he maybe really didn't notice his horse was gone."

Myles shook his head in disgust. "If that's the case, that's pretty serious neglect, to not even look after your horses for a day."

"Agreed." I paused. "I'm thinking of talking to him."

"Your neighbor? Bad idea. On a good day, he's unpleasant. I've had my own experience with his disagreeable nature. You start poking around about what happened to his horse, and you might encounter much worse than unpleasant."

"My aunt and uncle agree with you."

"But you're going to do it anyway, aren't you, headstrong girl."

"I don't know. I feel caution when three people whose opinion I respect advise against it. I'd like to get to the bottom of the mystery, if, indeed, *anyone* has murdered a horse."

We came to the corner of Myles' fenced property, and he could go no further. I reigned in Grifter.

"Be careful, Joy," Myles said, looking genuinely concerned. "There's no need to endanger yourself."

"Oh, I agree with you. I'm not inclined to be endangered! I'll pick Charley's brain and see what I can learn. If the horse is not to be found—whether stolen or done away with—I'll have to come up with some other companion for Grifter. Anything to distract him from that awful whining."

"Get another sheep."

"Yes. Maybe even that one that Uncle Eben gave to Lucy. I'm not above trying to coerce her into returning the little sheep."

"That's the best option, Joy. Set all this concern about the black stallion aside, and solve the problem with the obvious answer. Occam's Razor, shortest, most logical solution is to get Grifter a little friend he's already lived with."

Both of the horses started to fidget. Like little kids, they were getting bored standing at the corner of Myles' fence line.

"Well," Myles said, "Gotta get at some chores. I don't know what inspired me to go for a ride this morning when I have so much to do."

"I guess to have a chat with me," I laughed.

"So it seems." Myles reined Amber around.

"It was good to see you, Myles."

"Good to see you, too, Joy." He pulled Amber to a stop. "Say, there's a big hootenanny tomorrow evening at the Smith's barn. Why don't you come?"

"Oh!" That sounded like fun, and, more to the point, I might find out more about the neighbor's missing horse, chatting with the locals. "I don't want to crash their party."

"Come as my guest."

WHAT? "What about Sharon?" That pesky detail of a wife.

"She left me," he said, spurring Amber into a trot. "Be at my place at six if you decide to go," he called back on the breeze.

Chapter 6
Charley the Vet

Taking a few moments to recover from the shock, I finally shook the reins, and Grifter and I moved on. Sharon—who had stolen Myles away from me when I went off to college and he had to stay home to take care of the farm—had left him.

Did I want to know more about the story? Of course. Sort of. Grifter clopped along while I dug deeper into thought, until I got to Charley's veterinary practice, which was also his farm. With an add-on to the house for his smaller patients, and the barn for larger ones, it was quite the set-up.

I decided to check out the barn first, and sure enough, there he stood, attending to a goat.

"Hey, Charley," I said.

Looking over his shoulder, he smiled. "Hey, Joy! I think I can guess why you're here."

"I'm sure you can. And I'm on him." I chuckled.

"He seems happy enough." Charley led the little goat into a stall and came back to me as I dismounted. He patted Grifter and Grifter whinnied softly. He liked his doctor!

"Yes," I said. "He's happy as long as I'm here. But I have to get back to Oklumin and my work. The issue of the horrible noise he makes, and, more to the point, how unhappy he is when he's making it is a problem that must be solved."

Charley nodded somberly.

"Uncle Eben said Grifter formed a bond with a neighboring horse, and when the horse disappeared recently, Grifter started making that impossible sound."

"That seems to be the chain of events," Charley agreed.

"And, apparently, there are two thoughts about his disappearance. He was stolen or ... or ... done away with. Horrible thought."

"It's a horrible thought. But ... a possibility."

"What about the horse's identity chip?"

"He didn't have one. He hadn't yet gotten one when Dudley purchased him, and Dudley didn't want to pay for one."

"Weird," I mused, trying to understand yet another impractical move on the part of this Dudley dunderhead.

"No argument from me. I can suggest things, but I can't *make* people do things."

"This Dudley person becomes more and more unpleasant, the more I hear. However, I'm thinking about having a chat with him. He moved in a couple of years ago and I've never had an opportunity to talk with him. But his report card is, thus far, failing in every regard."

"And not likely to improve from me. His creatures are my patients, so I'm not going to say much about him. But, more importantly, I care about *you*, Joy, and I strongly recommend that you not go onto his property without his permission."

"*Yikes!* Charley, that's pretty strong."

"Heed my words, Joy, please. Just ... do that, will you?"

"You've sobered up my cocky internal conversation about being able to talk with this guy and not care what he says if he's rude. But what you suggest is a different can of worms."

"Yes. An entirely different can of worms." He snapped his fingers. "But wait! Here's an idea. I'm not aiding and abetting you now, but if you really want to talk with Dudley Garvy, the Smiths are having a barn party tomorrow night, and Dudley is likely to be there."

"Really?" I said, surprised. "That's counter-intuitive. Everyone seems to dislike him. Myles said he's 'unpleasant on a good day.' Why would he go to a casual barn party of people he's been rude to?"

"The guy is excessively class conscious. He's unpleasant to people he considers beneath him, and a sycophant with anyone he deems powerful, or that he can use to his benefit. And I've now said more than I should—still all under the flag of being concerned about you."

"Shoot-er-roonie, Charley, this Dudley's a real charmer, ain't he?" I shook my head. "No response necessary. Myles mentioned the hootenanny. I told him I didn't want to crash the party."

"I'm sure your aunt and uncle have been invited. In any case, the Smiths would love to see you."

"That's nice to hear." I mulled the whole thing over for a moment—but it needed more, and serious, mulling. Too much input in a mere hour.

"I'll probably go, especially with your added info. I don't suppose my aunt or uncle will go. But I might, anyway." I didn't mention that Myles had invited me to go with him. That was a conversation too big for this particular moment.

I turned to climb back onto Grifter, but paused. "Just to confirm, Grifter is okay? I mean, he's in good health?"

Charley scratched Grifter under his forelock. "He's great! His heart is strong, his teeth are good, his legs are perfect. And he has a sweet nature."

"He does, that. A big, lumbering, sweetie. And he has great lungs, if the ability to make a huge, unnatural sound indicates as much."

"Yes. His lungs are also in great shape. I suggested to your uncle that he get another animal as a companion for Grifter. He's a social creature. Well, all horses are social. I remember thinking it was a pity when your uncle gave away those sheep."

"He's regretting it now. But ... wouldn't it be great to find out where that beautiful black stud is? As long as he's not been murdered. I don't really want to know that." I got back on Grifter.

"It *would* be great. He's a beautiful animal who has sired a number of impressive foal. I'm hoping he turns up alive and unharmed."

I waved as I ambled out of the barn. "Me too. See you tomorrow, maybe, Charley."

"Hope so!"

I headed back to the home place, and even spurred Grifter into a bit of a run on the open road, which he seemed to enjoy as much as I did. We raced back to the barn. I took off his saddle and bridle and gave him a good currying, with lots of pets and hugs, and, finally, went into the house.

Aunt Claudia stood over the old-fashioned stove, stirring a big pot. The kitchen was redolent with the aroma of homemade vegetable soup, made with produce from Uncle Eben's garden.

Heaven!

"That was a pretty long ride," Aunt Claudia noted with her usual edge of disapproval.

Uncle Eben came in the back door. "It was—but such a beautiful day!"

"An absolutely scrumptious day!" I washed my hands at the kitchen sink and started to set the table. "Grifter and I ran into Myles and Amber, and we all had a lovely chat."

I watched as Aunt Claudia and Uncle Eben exchanged a look. In it I could read all the recent news. Namely, that Sharon had left Myles. I knew they wondered if Myles told me. I wanted to say then and there, "Yes, he told me Sharon left him." But I restrained myself. I did *not* want to get into that conversation. And besides, I was hungry, and much more interested in a big steaming bowl—maybe two! —of homemade soup.

"I hope we're intending to eat like, *right now*, because I'm hungry! I don't know when I smelled such a lovely soup."

"The bread will be ready in ten minutes," Aunt Claudia said. "Do you think you can wait that long?"

"Homemade bread, too? I'll wait!"

Soon, I sat hunkered over a great bowl of soup, accompanied by homemade bread. And not only that, after Uncle Eben got rid of the cows years previously, he bought a device that made the loveliest margarine with plant materials from his garden. Probably the most modern device on the property, even though it was now ten years old. I slathered my bread with the creamy margarine.

"So anyway, Myles mentioned this hootenanny tomorrow night at the Smith's barn. Are you going?"

"Oh, *pah!*" Aunt Claudia said. "You know I don't go in for that sort of thing."

"Right. That sort of thing. Music, laughter, conversation, dancing, fabulous food. Terrible! Just awful! Who would want to go to that?"

Aunt Claudia took my teasing surprisingly well. "For you, maybe. For me it's noisy, I have to come up with mindless conversation that I'm not interested in, dancing I can't do with my arthritis, and if your wolf-like manners are any indication of your opinion of my cooking, you appear to think I'm capable of making perfectly good food. I don't have to go elsewhere for it."

"*Verrrrrry* excellent food, Auntie. Which you could pack up and share with others and get more kudos than my paltry little comments."

"I don't need kudos from others."

"Well, *I* want to go, and, more to the point, I *need* to go. After chatting with Myles, I went to Charley's. Boy, has his spread expanded since the last time I visited him! A little goat was getting the best of his attention when I rode up. Anyway, it's now four for four, total agreement from everyone against my talking to your unpleasant neighbor about his missing horse.

"However! Charley said that he believes Mr. Unpleasant will likely turn up at the party, because, I guess, he has a penchant for social climbing. What better way to casually—and safely!—talk with him than at such an event?"

Aunt Claudia shook her head disapprovingly. "What do you think you'll accomplish by that?"

"It remains to be seen. True, it might be a failed experiment. But, on another hand, I might discover something that clears up the mystery of the missing horse." I paused to shovel a big hunk of bread into me—*oh, yum!* "Are you absolutely-positively-certain-sure that you will not come, Aunt Claudia?"

"Pretty darn certain."

"Then you won't mind if I recruit my uncle to escort me to the ball."

"*Harumph!*"

"How is that spelled?" I asked, grinning.

"Your uncle doesn't want to go to that shindig."

"Actually..." Uncle Eben dared to say, "It'd be my pleasure to be Joy's escort to 'that shindig.'"

"Well, I never!" Aunt Claudia uttered with a combination of shock and disdain.

"Even if you never, you could now!" I teased.

"No, I'm not going to now, either." She stood up and fussed around at the stove, though there was nothing there to fuss with. Uncle Eben and I had thrown her a curveball, and she didn't know what to do with it. "You'd better take two cars. When your uncle is bored after twenty minutes, you'll be frustrated to have to come home."

"Oh, I'm not worried about finding a ride home. Not one little bit. If Uncle Eben discovers it's not his cup of bluegrass, then he's welcome to come home. In fact, I'll drive, and he can even have my car bring him home."

I really didn't need Uncle Eben to go with me, I go to things by myself all the time. But—if Uncle Eben came with me, it took care of my trying to decide if I'd go over to Myles' place, discover he really didn't mean his invitation, or some other awkward revelation. While, conversely, going to the hootenanny alone would seem a bit rude, after he'd asked me to go with him.

But going with my uncle fixed both problems, because nobody knew better than Myles the tight rein my aunt had on Uncle Eben. He'll probably grin bigger than I am right now, seeing the two of us come through the door of the barn of the Smith's hootenanny.

I found that picture quite compelling and suddenly looked forward to tomorrow evening, when all day it had been a burdensome thought.

Now I'd really need those shiny, red, new-old boots of mine, hiding out in the dark recesses of my childhood closet.

Chapter 7

Red Boots

I spent the rest of the day puttering around in the garden with Uncle Eben, while Grifter, his head hanging over the garden fence, whinnied and otherwise engaged in our conversation.

It went like this: "Wow, these potatoes are huge, don't you think so, Grifter?"

Whereupon Grifter would make an agreeable sound. Then, Uncle Eben would say, "I'm looking forward to tomorrow night, Joy. It'll be a lot of fun. What do you think, Grifter?"

And Grifter neighed with enthusiasm.

We three shared a delightful afternoon that stretched into dusk. I watched as the evening shadows crept across the garden. Aunt Claudia's flowers at one end of the garden with a superabundance of aromatic flowers washed over me with a melody of aromas and colors that added to the impeccable day.

One might think that my uncle and I spent a lot of time engaged in conversation about the neighbor and his missing horse. But one would be wrong. Neither of us had an inclination to talk about anything negative. Instead, we shared reminiscences of when I was a little girl, and Uncle Eben and I spent many hours planning, planting, and harvesting the garden.

Happy days among many that were not.

* *

Saturday arrived, and, although I probably ought to have spent the day sorting out where the missing stallion might be, instead I spent the day sorting out what I would wear to the "casual" barn party.

Right. Care to guess what a "cowgirl" outfit is likely to cost? Take an estimate and multiply by ten. But such would not be the case for me tonight. I'd be wearing—if I could find them and they fit— my beautiful red boots from high school, the blue jeans I brought with me and wore all day yesterday, and, I hoped, one of Uncle Eben's plaid shirts, if one that fit could be found, as Aunt Claudia was not, and had never been, into wearing a western motif. Simple cotton dresses were her uniform of the day.

I knew I'd better get up before my aunt started calling me lazy, and I knew I should put some time in on the Kashmir project. But I didn't want to do either. I wanted to loll in bed, as if I was on some kind of vacation.

It seemed strange that I didn't hear any stirring in the house. After all, it was six-thirty a.m., long past the time they were usually up and running. I slipped out of bed and poked my head out my bedroom door.

Not a peep!

I tip-toed into the kitchen. *Nothing!* No oatmeal on the stove, no teapot singing.

They were still in bed! Oh, times have changed in the Forest household!

I went back into my little bedroom, but wide awake I no longer felt like lolling. I chuckled, thinking I could tease Aunt Claudia about being lazy.

I wouldn't, of course.

Unless I did, of course.

They no longer had to get up with the first crow of the rooster. They'd put in their time, and they deserved to take it easy. I reasoned this out as I went into my closet and prepared to start digging for the red boots. What a delight to discover the big boot box on the floor, right in front of me! And there too, much to my surprise, I discovered, neatly hanging, my childhood clothes.

How strange to see these clothes—in pristine condition and arranged chronologically, since I was nine years old. I thumbed through the hangers at the 'high school end,' hoping to find a cowgirl shirt. But for some strange reason, there was not one plaid shirt to be had.

All righty, then, back to counting on Uncle Eben's closet for a shirt, I focused my attention on the boot box. I took the box back to my bed, sat cross-legged on the bed, preparing to open the box, and was about to talk to Robbie about my excitement about the boots, when I realized he wasn't here.

I missed him!

I opened the boot box, and there before me, wrapped carefully in tissue, I discovered my beautiful red boots, looking as if they'd just come off the showroom shelf.

Would they fit? I took one out of the box and turned to sit on the edge of the bed, slipping the boot over my bare foot. *Perfect! Perfect! Perfect!*

I grabbed up my wrist comp and projected a 3-D into the room connecting with my bedroom at home.

"Robbie," I called. He popped up on the bed. "What were you doing?"

"Oh! Hi Joy! Wow! It's great to see you!"

His enthusiasm seemed a bit over the top, given that it had only been a couple days since he saw me. Suspecting he might have been into a bit of mischief, I let it go for the moment. "I thought I'd show you my much-treasured childhood boots."

"The red boots! Yes? The red boots!"

"You know about my red boots?" I asked, mystified.

"Of course, you've told me about them more than once."

"Really? When?"

"Do you want me to call up the verbal record, Joy?"

"No, no, not necessary. But ... I don't recall talking to you about my red boots. Anyway, here they are." I held the one up that wasn't on my foot for him to see.

"It's beautiful! Are you bringing them home with you?"

"Well, Robbie, this is home too, so ... no... I'll be leaving them here." For some reason, the thought that Aunt Claudia had kept my clothes, especially the red boots ... well, I had to assume they were important to her. Which I would never-never-never have guessed.

"Okay then, leave the boots there. But, bring yourself back!"

"I'll be back, don't worry."

"And when is that?"

"Not too sure at this precise moment, Robbie. I'm in the midst of a mystery."

"How does this always happen with you? Everywhere you go, you come upon a mystery."

My Goodness! I'd never thought of it, but what Robbie said seemed to be nearly true. "Well, Robbie, I think there's mysteries everywhere. Most people don't bother to notice them. And even if they do, they're not inclined to solve them. I don't come up with mysteries, I'm just attuned to them."

Robbie furrowed his furry brow. "*Verrry* interesting, Joy. I'm going to contemplate what you said for a while after you disconnect."

"Which I'm about to do right now."

"You're not going to tell me about the mystery?" Robbie asked, stunned.

"No, I'm not. It's too complicated, and I haven't quite thought it through yet. But! I *will* tell you that I'm going to a hootenanny tonight."

"Hootenanny," Robbie said reflectively. I could tell he was shuffling through his dictionary. 'An informal gathering with bluegrass music, fiddle playing, and dancing.' *Ohhhhhh...* It sounds like *so much fun*. I wish I was there."

I tried to picture my mid twenty-first century robot cat at what would be a mid-twentieth century party. The picture would not gel. "I'll try to remember to let you see a bit of it, discreetly. It, candidly, would spook some of these folks half to death to see a talking cat hovering in their midst."

"*Noooooo!* I wouldn't want to spook anyone half to death. Why would I scare them?"

"Because many of them may not even know that there's such a thing as a robot cat, let alone actually seeing one talk like a human. In their midst. On a holo."

"I ... I ... I don't know what to say!"

"Don't let it upset you, Robbie. It's you and me, kitty, all the way! We don't need anyone else. And Dickens. How is Dickens?" Changing the subject so, hopefully, Robbie would not become depressed, as this was a delicate component of his programming.

"He's great! Here on the bed sleeping as always, so entertaining, lots of fun. Can't wait to play the sleep game some more with my favorite cat."

"My, my, Robbie, you've really developed your ability to be sarcastic. But, my dear furry friend, you could wake him up and make him get a bit of exercise, it wouldn't be all bad."

"Oh. I could do that? You wouldn't mind if I woke Dickens up and played with him?"

"No, not as long as you don't do it too much. You know, he's bio, and not a young cat anymore. So be thoughtful and don't overdo it."

"All right. I won't overdo it. But that does help with the boredom factor."

"Conversely, I could have you go to sleep."

"No, no, no, Joy, no need to do that."

How he hated it when I commanded him to sleep. Anyway, I needed him awake and guarding our modest little castle, and taking care of Dickens. "Okay then, Robbie dear, be good, have fun, and I'll see you soon."

He waved a paw as I shut off the holo.

"Who in heaven's name are you talking to?" Aunt Claudia asked from the other side of my door.

Chapter 8

Dressing for the Ball

"Come on in, Auntie."

She stepped into the room.

"Lookie," I said, holding up my foot with the red boot. "The boots fit perfectly." I took it off and put it back in the box. "To answer your question, I was talking with my robot cat, checking in to make sure everything is okay there, and telling him a bit about what I'm up to here."

"You're talking to a robot cat as if it's a person." She shook her head in vexation.

"Not only as if he's a person, but as if he's a cherished companion and friend. Which he is."

"It's a machine."

"True. Sort of. Robbie has bio-components. He learns how to interact with me by … interacting with me. He knows my likes and dislikes. He guards my home, takes care of my bio cat, Dickens when I'm not there, allowing me to be here without worrying about him or having to bring him. Robbie helps keep the house clean and organized, and on and on …."

Aunt Claudia's brow wrinkled. "*Hmmmm,*" she muttered softly. "It sounds like I need a Robbie."

I laughed. "There you go! That's a great idea. You don't have to get a cat. You could get a German Shepard, for instance, to guard the place."

Aunt Claudia shuddered. "A talking German Shepherd would be … spooky. Somehow, a talking cat is a bit more acceptable." She shook her head, as if trying to release the entire picture. "Anyway, coming into present reality, you don't still intend to go to that what's-it tonight, do you?"

"I surely do!" I said, surprised. "I found my lovely boots, I have the jeans I've been wearing since I got here. I dug through the closet in the hopes of finding an acceptable plaid shirt, but couldn't find a single one. By the way, the way you've kept and organized my childhood clothes is quite touching."

Aunt Claudia looked away from me and out the window. "Well, I didn't know if you would want them or not. But, I don't have anything else to put in that space, so why not organize them?"

"Yes, well, it provided an interesting little trip down memory lane. But I'm surprised not to see even one plaid shirt. I must have had at least a couple worth keeping."

"You had a dozen nice Western shirts. I sold them. All in one fell swoop, to a woman absolutely delighted to have them."

I chuckled wryly. So much for sentiment, when pitted against money. This was more like the aunt I remember. "I hope you took that trip to Paris with the money, dear Aunt."

"Trip to Paris? What are you saying? I have no inclination of going to Paris, for pity's sake!"

"I know, Aunt Claudia. I'm trying to be funny. Failed experiment. But, now, what do I wear tonight? We must raid Uncle Eben's closet after he gets up."

"He's up. He's been up for a while. He's outside puttering around doing, whatever it is that he does when he goes outside and putters around."

I jumped up from the bed. "Excellent. Let's see what he's got that I can maybe wear tonight."

"Really, Joy, I cannot understand why you would even want to go to that thing."

"Strangely enough, I'm not in your skin. And the person in *my* skin enjoys an occasional party. Not only that, there's a mystery to be solved." I threw on the housecoat I'd found in the closet and herded Aunt Claudia out of my room and down the hall to their room. "And remember, my goal is to sort out either where that big beautiful black stallion might be, or, failing that, at least, perhaps come up with another creature that would be a good companion for Grifter."

"Well, yes, that's a goal worth pursuing," Aunt Claudia said as she open the door to their bedroom.

I could tell by the shift in her voice that she'd now been recruited to the notion of my going to the hootenanny—if it meant Grifter would cease whining—making my whole day easier.

We went to their closet. I honestly don't think I've ever been in it in my life! The small walk-in closet held all of Aunt Claudia's clothes on the right on one clothes pole, and Uncle Eben's clothes on the left on two tiers, shirts on the top, and pants on the bottom.

It surprised me how many clothes he had! All lovely and beautifully cared for, pressed and smelling fresh. Aunt Claudia pulled half a dozen shirts off the closet pole and brought them out into the bedroom, arraying them on the bed, which, I couldn't help but notice, was neatly made. Not a common site in bed-rooms where I resided.

I immediately picked out the predominantly purple plaid shirt with a thin red thread running through it. It would go perfectly with my long-in-storage boots. A beautiful gold cord emphasized the shirt's Western styling, with deep purple snaps down the front and on the cuffs.

As beautiful as I found the shirt to be, I also thought it was quite feminine. I restrained myself from saying as much, however. "What do you think about this one for me, Aunt Claudia?" I held it up and turned to look in the full-length mirror on the closet door.

"I think it's perfect for you! I don't like that shirt on your uncle. It's too girly. He bought it himself one day when left to his own devices."

"*Heavens!* What were you thinking, letting him out on his own?"

"Despite your hyperbole, Joy, the day he went out on his own has proven to be beneficial for you, has it not?"

I couldn't quite tell if she was playing along, or upset. I decided to tread softly. "Anyway, I can see why he bought this shirt because, despite its rather feminine appearance, it is truly beautiful. And exceptionally well made," I noted. I looked at the label. "Where did he get a *MacWestern Outfitters'* shirt around here?"

"Oh, I didn't even notice that! It must've cost a small fortune! If I recall correctly, and it's been several years, that was the day he went to Seattle. Interesting. I think he wore the shirt a total of one time."

"No doubt, if you commented on it being 'girly.' But I bet, behind your back every now and then, he pulls this shirt out of the closet and looks at it longingly." What was the matter with me? Could I not stop being sardonic?

Ahm, no. I guess not. Interestingly, my aunt seemed willing to play along. She nodded in agreement. I have only one question for the Universe: *What have you done with my aunt?*

I headed back to my room. "What to wear was the biggest dilemma for me today, which is now beautifully resolved," I said. Just to be sure that it fit, though I felt certain it would as my uncle and I were nearly the same size, and I had worn his hand-me-downs in high school to do chores, I slipped on the beautiful shirt and looked in the mirror.

Whoa! This was no doing-chores-hand-me-down shirt. I'd be the belle of the hootenanny ball. It fit perfectly and looked fabulous.

It made me so happy, I started humming a Valtar Val tune, and I even made my little bed. I then laid the shirt out on the bed, with my boots at the foot.

Standing there, thinking about how unforeseen all these developments were, I could feel a riveting chain of events unfolding.

Chapter 9

Rootin'-Tootin' Hootenanny!

During breakfast, I confessed to my uncle that I had absconded with his most beautiful shirt. "Is that all right?"

"Yes, of course, Joy, any shirt of mine is yours!"

"Don't tell me that! You might end up without any western shirts!" I laughed, as I headed out the back door and went to the barn to hang out with Grifter.

I curried him, braided his mane, and rode him around the pasture bareback with only the halter and its single rein. We had a lovely, lazy, day together. I couldn't help but recall how desperately, as a teenager, I had wanted to get away from here. But now, this bucolic afternoon, being here didn't seem half bad at all.

Not half bad at all.

I spent the rest of my musings on looking forward to the evening's festivities with a calm anticipation. Whatever happened, I said to myself, I would enjoy myself. But, *most importantly*, my sixth sense told me, a companion for darling Grifter would be discovered.

After a bit of late lunch, I retired to my room to make myself presentable, and perhaps a bit more than merely presentable for the countryside hootenanny, with neighbors I haven't seen in a decade.

I even put on some eyeshadow that I found in the dresser drawer that I'd completely forgotten I ever had.

Given my aunt's disapproval of makeup in general, and flashy sparkly eyeshadow in particular, I was surprised to find it. It looked brand new, and I must have never used it. But I could see my younger self buying it and squirreling it away, just because I'd found it pretty. And, yay, Aunt Claudia had left it in the dresser drawer. How did it manage to be absolutely perfect for my spontaneous ensemble? Sparkly lavender, beautiful with the purple plaid western shirt.

After almost two hours of fussing with the pallet of my face and body, my uncle knocked timidly on the door. "Joy? Are you still alive?"

"Very, very much so, Uncle Eben." I looked at my wrist comp on the bedside table and saw that it was, *shockingly!* five-thirty, and time to go! "Wow! I didn't know it was so late. I got carried away with indulging myself. Give me a couple minutes, and I'll be right out."

I soon went out to the kitchen where the two of them sat over cups of tea, their eyes riveted on the hall down which I came.

Just call me catwalk Joy!

My uncle actually whistled, which I'm not sure I've ever heard him do in my life.

"You've made my shirt quite happy," he said, laughing as he stood. "Shall we go?"

"I'm ready if you are." I looked at my aunt. I could be wrong, but there seemed to be the slightest edge of wistfulness in her look. "You can still come with us, you know, Aunt Claudia. We can be fashionably late, I don't care."

"No, no. I know I would not enjoy myself. I don't like crowds. I'll enjoy it through your experience." She stood, picked up a bag and handed it to me. "You can take this with you."

I looked inside the bag and saw a decorative tureen, filled with the exquisite soup she'd made the day before, and that I knew she had intended to freeze for future meals.

"Oh, Aunt Claudia, this is wonderful. Thank you so much! I honestly forgot about taking something, though it would have hit me on the road, and I would've pulled in to the store to get something not nearly as fantastic as this."

I gave her a one-armed hug, then turned to my uncle. "I guess we'd better hit the road. Don't look for us until you see us!" We went out the front door to my car.

"We'll both ride in the back," I said as I put the tureen of soup on the front seat and commanded the car to lock it in with the safety belt.

"Okay, Joy. It's still something I have a hard time with, but it's perfectly safe, yes?"

"Safer than if you or I were driving, yes." He referred, of course, to the experience of the car driving itself. We got in the back. "Dale Smith's barn, please," I said to the car. "You've not been there yet, it's...."

"I have it," the car answered. "It's near Charley, the vet."

"That's right! Uncle Eben and I are going to chat, so don't be distracted by anything we might say."

"Noted," the car replied. "I shall respond only to your direct address."

We soon arrived at the Smith's festive barn, where people were arriving in droves. Human driven cars, self-driving cars, people on horseback, and people in horse-drawn carriages, reminiscent of a day *loooong* gone by. The outside of the big red barn, draped in brightly colored bunting, welcomed one and all.

Everyone had something in hand, and I was grateful that Aunt Claudia had given me the tureen of soup, which would stand out as a favorite, I felt certain, among the many dishes people brought.

Not even six p.m. yet, and I could hear fiddle playing from the car. I looked over at Uncle Eben, who grinned like a little boy. It warmed my heart to see him utterly blissful.

"Where would you like me to park, Joy?" the car asked.

"Not too close. We're both in good shape and can hike a bit, so leave the closest spaces for people who may need to be closer."

The car soon maneuvered into a space some distance from the barn.

"Perfect!" Uncle Eben declared. "So thoughtful of you, Joy. Honestly, the thought would not have crossed my mind. I'd have tried to get as close as I could. But why? Fortunately, I've got two good feet. You're absolutely right."

I started to get out of the car.

"Don't move!" Uncle Eben leapt from the car and hurried around it to open my door.

"Why, thank you, sir," I said, smiling. I offered him my hand, and stepped out of the car. I reached into the front seat to retrieve Aunt Claudia's tureen of soup. "I will call for you later," I said to the car.

"Noted," the car replied, shutting off its engine.

"Pretty nifty," Uncle Eben said with approval. "Do you think I should upgrade our old jalopy?"

"You could try. It's a bit old. My car is about the oldest car that can be self-drive retrofitted. But why not simply get a new car?"

"I'd be tempted," Uncle Eben said as we made our way to the barn. "But I'm sure we can both agree that your aunt is highly unlikely to be interested in a self-driving car. We don't go anywhere much, anyway."

"*Ummm*," I muttered noncommittally. The thought that they were getting older and might be safer if they had a self-driving car took my mind for the moment. I'd have to see if I couldn't come up with a project to generate enough extra income to finance such a project.

But now the music of country bluegrass, swelling like audio balloons from the cheerful barn, blocked further conversation.

When was the last time I'd been to a party? Over the previous year, I'd been to a few professional events pegged as "parties," more like grueling experiences of meaningless small talk, peppered among efforts of people trying to manipulate one another.

Guess what? Not my definition of a party.

But this was!

As we entered through the broad doorway of the barn, I saw a long table laden with culinary delights in the subdued light. I placed my aunt's soup tureen among them.

The musicians played at the far end of the barn, on a temporary stage. People milled about, smiling and greeting one another. My eyes adjusted to the muted light of lanterns, which looked like live flame, although I doubted it.

I became a bit overwhelmed at the thought that I was about to see people I hadn't seen in over a decade.

Yes, the thought had passed through my mind, but now the "realness" of it made me feel a bit anxious. Yes, from time to time when I visited my aunt and uncle I'd see somebody I knew when we went shopping, which was rare enough. But tonight I'd encounter a large dose of my childhood. Was I ready for it?

I knew people would recognize me, not because they actually recognized me, but because I was with my uncle. I turned to him and said softly, "Uncle Eben, be sure to mention the name of people when they come up to us, as I may not recognize them. They'll know me because I'm with you. I'm trying to avoid being embarrassing."

"Good point," he whispered back. Then chuckled. "Let's hope I can remember their names! We may both get to be embarrassed."

I laughed. "Oh well, all in good fun! I'm sure everyone will be forgiving. In fact, they may know who I am, but not be able to remember my name."

"Not remember Joy? That would be terrible—no one should ever forget joy!"

That was one of the things I particularly loved about my name. Certainly, one had to at least subliminally feel joy when hearing or saying my name. A philosophy I have is that there are two main reasons for living: *LOVE* and *JOY*.

But enough philosophizing! I came here to party, and to find a companion for Grifter, in reverse order of importance. Hoping for a red hot trail to the missing black stallion, who had now been at large about five days now, if I understood correctly.

"Hey, Eben," an elderly man came up and patted my uncle on the back. I recognized him immediately as one of my elementary school teachers, Mr. Johnson. Yes, he looked a bit older, and yet he looked the same!

"Mr. Johnson!" I exclaimed, "It's wonderful to see you!"

He peered at me for a few moments. "Joy? Is it little Joy?"

"Not so little," Uncle Eben interjected, "at nearly six feet."

"True," Mr. Johnson agreed. "But Joy, I've been following your amazing work. Not only are you doing an important job of preserving culture, but you do it with flair and humor."

Shocked to discover that anyone here would know anything about what I do, I was immensely flattered. "But Mr. Johnson, I would not have been successful, if not for your brilliant teaching in English class. You taught me how to communicate clearly while keeping my personality in my writing."

It was a mega bonus for the evening to see my childhood teacher, who'd instrumental in my becoming a writer and research scientist.

"Thank you, dear, for that compliment," he said. "But I think that now you may refer to me as John."

"Happily," I said.

"Unless, of course, you would prefer I address you as 'Dr. Forest.'"

"Oh, heavens no! Please don't do that." I laughed.

As we shared a comradely chuckle, two women came rushing up to our little trio. *"Joy! Joy!"* they called.

Oh, no, I thought, now it begins! People I don't know who know me.

Chapter 10

Great Friends, Horrible Neighbor

But no! I recognized them right off, as soon as I could make them out in the subdued light. Bonny and Betty. They were best friends in high school, and also, pretty good friends of mine.

"Bonny and Betty—look at you, still hanging out together," I exclaimed.

Group hug! The two of them babbled a rush of greetings, talking over one another. I grinned. They hadn't changed one little bit. Well, yes, they had each put on, *ahem*... forty-ish pounds. But who's looking? Not me! They both had their long brown hair in braids, and they wore matching western shirts, Bonny's pink, and Betty's a pale green.

"I'm chatting with Mr. err, with John," I said, "better known to me as Mr. Johnson."

"Hi John," Betty and Bonny said together.

"Hi, you two mischief makers. Are you not in detention today?"

They both giggled girlishly. "We snuck out," Bonny said, "We know we're in big trouble, but we couldn't miss this party!"

"It's wonderful to see you! You remember my Uncle Eben?"

"Of course!" they chorused. "Hello, Mr. Forest."

"Eben, please, dear ladies."

"Oh yes, please," I agreed. "Informal is the key phrase for the evening."

"Absolutely, yes!" Betty gushed. "Informal, and dancing and *food!*" She made a sweeping gesture at the long table beside us.

"Yes!" I nodded. "More food than I've seen in one place in quite a while. There's nothing like going to the country to be well-fed."

"So true!" Bonny patted her stomach. "Well-fed, and over-fed."

"But that's three children, not just food," Betty said, defending her friend.

"Three children—rascals running around here somewhere, and number four on the way."

"Oh! Bonny! Really?" Betty exclaimed gleefully.

Bonny nodded with a Mona Lisa smile.

"Congratulations," Uncle Eben said.

Dumbfounded, I couldn't even faintly imagine having three children, "with a fourth on the way."

"That's so amazing," I sort of whispered, trying, still, to conceptualize having several children.

"Here's the sperm donor now," Bonny laughed as a tall, bald man ambled up to us. That's when I noticed that the tall, bald man was none other than little Richie Collins, who had been my next-door neighbor when we were in grade school. His family moved away when we got into high school, but apparently he'd managed to find Bonny again.

"Hey, Hon," he leaned down and kissed his co-child-maker on the cheek.

"Lookie, Richie, lookie who's here!" She put her arm around my shoulders.

Richie looked blankly at me.

"It's Joy Forest," she prompted. "Goodness, you two were neighbors for years."

"*Oh! Oh! Joy!*" To my shock, he grabbed me in a bear hug. "*Wow!* You're gorgeous!" He turned and grinned at his wife. "Not quite as gorgeous as Bonny, but pretty darn gorgeous."

Bonny giggled. "Always a flirt!"

"It's true," Richie agreed. "Jeez, Joy, I had such a crush on you when I was that shy, goofy kid."

"You did?" News to me!

"Yep. That is, until Bonny took my heart. You might say she seduced me away from you. Back in third grade, one day she and I happened to be walking somewhere after school, the bus stop, or candy shop, or whatever, and I confessed to her my infatuation with you. And she said, 'Richie, you are not in Joy's league. She's beyond your reach. But I'm not.' And then, brave girl that she was, she kissed me. I was a goner, from that moment to this."

"My goodness," I said, taking in the surprising information. "I had no idea I'd learn all of this history tonight!"

Weirdly, my comment made everyone laugh boisterously, and, although bemused by why, I joined their contagious laughter.

"Wow, Bonny, that's amazing!" I said. "I could never have initiated kissing a boy when I was, how old were we then? Seven or eight? Goodness! You really knew what you wanted!"

"I did!"

"But," Richie said to his wife, "would you have kissed me if you'd known I'd lose all my hair in my mid-twenties?"

"You'd better believe it, baby!" she said over our guffaws. "I had my sights on you from the first day I saw you, when we were five years old!"

"*Awwww*," we sighed in unison. Richie grinned like that five-year-old boy.

And would it not happen that at that precise moment, the boy who would have been my 'sperm donor' had things been different, came up to our group. He had a girl in tow who looked so much like Sharon—bright red hair to her waist and huge green luminescent eyes—that it nearly knocked me for a loop.

"Joy! You came!" Myles exclaimed.

"I'm here! Discovering all about a ton of things going on around me as a kid that I knew nothing about!"

He gave me a small hug, then turned to my uncle and shook his hand. "Good to see you, Eben."

"It's great to see you too, Myles."

"So, what's the old-news that you didn't know?" he asked.

"Bonny and Richie were sharing with me their sweet romance, which began in grade school. You know, his family lived next to us at that time," I said.

"Vastly superior neighbors to the character Claudia and I have now," Uncle Eben added.

Bonny shuddered. "That...." she shook her head vehemently, "I cannot say in polite company what I think of that so and so."

"Oh? Why do you hate him?" I asked. "I've never met him. From what everyone says, I'm better off."

"He's a horrible person. I watched him slap one of his mares across the muzzle with the reins of her bridle, and swearing a blue streak under his breath when showing his horses at the state fair. I have no idea what made him go off on that sweet horse. She's the loveliest, gentlest roan I've ever met. When he left the horse stall, I went over and talked with her and petted her, poor thing. She had welts and a little bit of blood across her muzzle within centimeters of her eye."

"Did you report him?" I asked, aghast.

"Indeed I did report him to the fair board. But by the time they got around to check on her, the welt was gone, there was no blood. Undoubtedly, Mr. Gonzo, schmoozed them with some cash. As far as I'm concerned, he can just...."

Betty, standing by me, facing the opposite direction of Bonny, raised her eyebrows and nodded behind Bonny. "Here comes your favorite person now."

Approaching us came a large, impressive man, with a shock of black hair and large facial features; big eyes, big nose, big mouth. That last apparently applied to him in both physical and behavioral terms. He moved forcefully, as if against a tidal wave.

Taking in his weird, inauthentic smile, while still processing the intensity and the *horror* of Bonny's words, I became decidedly uncomfortable. I did not want to meet this vile person.

Chapter 11
Pacifica!

What kind of plonker would strike a horse across her face with *anything*, let alone leather reins, which would not only hurt, but could disfigure a show horse? Hateful *and* stupid person, by any definition.

I found myself cheering inwardly for whoever "rescued" the black stallion from him, while, again, hoping with all my heart that the horse had not been murdered.

As he joined our group, our jovial camaraderie was sucked out like air from a vacuum tube. Who in our little clutch of friends would he be angling to interact with? I wondered, recalling Charley's comment that "Mr. Gonzo" was a first class schmoozer. None of us were schmooze-worthy.

Right then, Charley came up to our group behind me. *Ah!* That was probably the person Mr. Gonzo intended to encounter. After all, Charley had grown a large operation, had saved many livestock animals and pets—or helped escort them to heaven—for everyone in the community, with compassion and great skill. He no doubt also had clout in the community.

"Hey, Charley," the interloper's voice boomed.

"Hello, Dudley."

"I knew I'd see you here! I guess you want to talk with these folks," his glance grazed over us without actually taking anyone in. "But I'd like to have a few minutes of your time before the evening's over."

"All right, Dudley, but no business talk. I'm off the clock!" Charley chuckled airily.

He impressed me with his beautifully cool manner, given that he may well know more about Dudley than the rest of us, combined.

"*Hah!*" Dudley exclaimed with a wooden sound. "Is there anything that's not business? But I'll try to keep it fun. Upcoming elections, you know." He turned to leave, as his glance again passed superficially over our group. Then he stopped, riveting his attention on me.

"Who is this charming siren?" He leered at me.

I couldn't help myself, I shrank back.

"This is my niece, Joy," Uncle Eben said, putting his arm protectively around me.

Dudley took a step back. "*You're* Joy Forest? Holy crap, brilliant *and* beautiful. No one ever mentioned you're a hot babe."

The immensity of my distaste prevented me from uttering a word. But both Bonny and my uncle rushed to my defense.

"Beautiful and brilliant yes, but hot babe?" Bonny said with undisguised dislike. "You're inappropriate, Dudley."

At the same moment, my uncle, quivering with anger, said in a low, dangerous voice I'd never heard, "Sir, you will kindly address my niece politely."

Dudley laughed as though he thought everyone was making a joke. "My, my, Miss Forest, ahem, I mean, *Dr. Forest*, you have your defenders! Still, I must say it's a privilege to meet you. I'm familiar with your work."

"*Really?*" Betty exclaimed. "*Why?*"

He raised his eyebrows in surprise. "Because she comes from this back water dump and has made a name for herself."

Sheesh! Had I ever encountered *anyone* with the capacity of being so insulting in such short order? And I'd been having such a good time! Now I had to deal with this nasty piece of work hitting on me, right in front of family and friends.

I watched as Myles' daughter—who I assumed the beautiful red-headed girl must be—turned her back on the group. I heard her softly say, *"Go away!"*

No one else seemed to hear her, but it was surely the sentiment of everyone in the group. And it worked!

"Nice chatting," Dudley said in his too-loud voice. "But I must be off. There's other folks I need to hook up with before the evening's over."

"Too bad for those other people," Betty muttered when he was out of earshot.

"Yes, well…." Charley began.

We all waited in breathless anticipation for his conclusion. When none came, we all giggled, and our previous mood returned.

"Quite the party killer," I noted.

"Yes. I just hope he's not also a horse killer," Uncle Eben said.

We murmured our agreement.

"What do you think, Charley?" he continued. "Could he have done away with that beautiful stallion? Bonny just told us about seeing him strike one of his mares violently across the muzzle. What would keep him from going further?"

Charley shook his head. "It's one thing to strike out in anger. Despicable, yes. But quite another thing to actually kill a horse, and then dispose of it. Dudley has a mountain of personality problems, he ought not have *any* animal, let alone high maintenance creatures such as horses. But, no, I don't think he killed the black stallion."

An immense relief poured through me, hearing his thoughtful opinion. He could be wrong, of course. But for the moment, I'd put my energy into his being correct.

"Besides that, what's he all up about, needing to talk with you?" Betty asked.

A small frown crossed Charley's features. "I ought to keep this to myself, but … *hmmm*, I'm not going to. He's planning on running for Mayor."

An exclamation of disbelief rose from the group.

"I can't see that he'll get anywhere with such a delusion, given that he's resoundingly disliked, if this group is any indication," I observed.

"He has supporters in other sectors of the community," John said. "He's been canvassing in my neighborhood and has won over quite a few potential votes. I don't understand what they see in him. He's so greasy, he left a spot on my welcome mat. I don't know why people don't see through this sort of person."

"Oh, jeez, you're too funny, John," I said, laughing. "But people are generally good, and they project this onto others. It's a huge problem with politics. Everyone wants a savior, but, really, we must save ourselves."

"You're *so right*, Joy," Myles agreed. "I'm still seething. How dare he speak to you in that way? I wanted to deck him."

"I wish you had, Dad," the red-headed girl piped up. "Let's go do it now. I'll hold him while you pound him!"

Myles put his arm around her. "The problem with that, my darling daughter, is we lower ourselves to his level. And we must stay above such characters."

"Amen," Uncle Eben mumbled.

"Well, enough ickiness about a distasteful person. Let us clear our palate by digging into this lovely bounty." I gestured to the ever-filling table.

"Yes," Betty seconded, "let's! Unpleasant neighbor, not good. Good food, *GOOD!*" She led the way to a stack of plates, which we filled to overflowing, then hunkered down on bales of straw to enjoy the feast.

I was happy when Betty shared a bale with me, rather than going off with her several children.

"It's really so delightful to see you, Betty."

"Me too you, Joy!"

I hesitated to ask her the question I had on the top of my mind. One never knew if the answer would be another one of those unpleasant topics. But I charged ahead. "So, dare I ask—where's your significant other?"

"You *do* dare ask! And thank you! I'm married to James Walzer. Do you remember him? He's a couple years older than we are. He's *so* amazing. He's working on building the off-shore city, Pacifica. Can you believe it? It's quite an honor. Only the best science minds and contractors were chosen for this massive project. I'm so proud of him! Though, at the same time, the kids and I miss him terribly. He's out there three months at a time, then home for a month."

I was shocked. "Oh, Betty, that's astounding! Of course I remember James. I remember he won every science prize to be had, and scholarships, too, if I recall correctly."

"True. All true. He's brilliant. And still manages to be adorable." She grinned, but I couldn't miss the edge of sadness in her expression.

"To be chosen to work on Pacifica, that's beyond outstanding!"

She nodded, smiling softly. "I'm glad you understand. There are those ... even, maybe, one's best friend, who do not understand the honor, and think he ought to be home with his family. True, he's not here for every school game or school production in person. But he's nearly always with us via holo. And, yes, it's a great honor. Pacifica will go down in human history as one of our age's greatest achievements."

"Indeed, it will. And...." I hesitated.

"And what?"

"Well, I've been trying to figure out how I can wrangle a pass to visit Pacifica. As an ethnographer documenting the times I live in, I need to spend some time there. It's a treasured project of mine to produce a detailed record in words, images and holos of the construction of the first major city in the ocean. Do you think James could help me get a pass?"

"What a wonderful idea, Joy. People need to understand Pacifica better than they do, and you'd make it fascinating. I'll talk with him. Maybe he can even sponsor you."

"That would be phenomenal!" I kept my over-the-top excitement down to a quiet roar. But inside myself, I jumped up and down with glee. How I wanted to go to Pacifica! Yet another totally unanticipated bonus for this trip to the home village.

Fabulous evening, and it had only just begun! However, the primary assignment still loomed heavily. "I don't suppose you know of anyone who has a sheep or some animal that might keep my horse, Grifter, company?"

Betty looked at me, mystified. "How does that relate....?"

"*Sorry!* It doesn't. As important as this news about Pacifica is—and *it is*—my immediate problem is finding a companion for Grifter, if 'Mr. Gonzo's' beautiful black stallion cannot be found, or has otherwise been ... anyway, Grifter had formed an across-the-fence friendship with that beautiful stud, and now, with him missing, Grifter is braying like a donkey, only worse. That's why I'm here. Aunt Claudia called and threatened to sell Grifter if he didn't stop making that noise."

"She wouldn't dare!"

"No, she really wouldn't. Or. rather, couldn't. But poor Grifter! He's so depressed. Uncle Eben said he'd been happy with the three sheep, but my aunt insisted they were an unnecessary expense, so he gave them away. Now my dear Grifter needs a companion."

"*Awww*, poor horsie! Every creature needs a companion. I'll keep my eyes and ears open. If I come up with anything, I'll let you know!"

"Thank you so much, Betty!"

"You're entirely welcome, dear friend," she replied.

Myles came up to us. "Let's dance, Joy!"

Oh, no! I said to my little pitter-pattering heart.

Chapter 12

Bluegrass Dance

"No, no, Myles. I ... ah, no."

He looked hurt. It must have taken courage to ask me to dance, but it would take more courage on my part to dance with him.

"Why not?" he pressed.

"Yeah," Betty entered the fray, "why not? You're the one who said you wanted to party, so get up and dance, darn it!" She teasingly pushed at me. "You've got your red boots on, so get up and," she broke into song, "dance the blues."

"Jeezarini, Betty, you have an incredible voice! You ought to be on the stage."

"I may, later. But you're not changing the subject so easily, young woman. I'll sing a song later if you'll dance now." She looked up at Myles and winked.

"I'm being pressured," I complained.

"Yes, you are." Betty took my plate, then Myles took my hands, pulling me to stand.

"Betty!" one of the musicians called from the stage, "come on up and sing!"

She plopped her plate and mine on the end of the table, piling up with used plates, and scurried to the stage.

As Betty began to belt out an upbeat song, Myles, still holding my hand, led me to the sawdust covered and crowded dance area.

"I'm going to embarrass you," I protested. "I don't know these dances."

"You can't embarrass me, Joy. We won't do any of these dances—we'll find our own little spot here on the edge."

Oh, yes, Myles and I had been quite the country dance couple in high school. But I'd never been to a bluegrass venue since then.

Since he broke my heart.

He took me in his arms, and, much to my surprise, my feet knew what they were doing as long-fallow dance moves surfaced. Soon we were spinning around the dance floor as if we did this every weekend. Everyone and everything whirled around us in a kaleidoscope of muted light and colors. I found myself grinning like the schoolgirl I used to be.

Betty's song came to an end, and Myles and I stood there, catching our breath. I looked around me —there in the nearby shadows at the edge of the stage, I saw Uncle Eben hunkered down over a chessboard with one of his cronies.

Oh, that made me happy! Seeing him enjoying himself with a friend was worth the entire evening.

He looked up. Seeing Myles and me standing nearby, a lighthearted smile crossed his features.

"Your uncle approves," Myles said.

"So it seems. But isn't it lovely to see him enjoying himself with one of his pals? I didn't know he played chess! I wonder if he's good at it."

"You'll have to ask him." Myles took a step back and took me in from head to foot. Inwardly, I wriggled uncomfortably. Outwardly, I remained calm as a cucumber. Or so I told myself. "You look fantastic, Joy. And the red boots! They're like new."

"That's one thing I can say about my Aunt Claudia. She takes great care of things. You should see my closet! Imagine my surprise to discover my clothes from when I was a little girl to the time I left home, in chronological order neatly hung in my tiny childhood closet. So, when I saw my clothes there, I expected to find at least one of my western shirts. But I could not find one scrap of plaid!"

"What happened to them?" Myles asked, surprised. "You had beautiful western shirts."

"I know! Well, they were *so* beautiful that my aunt sold them, one and all. She did not keep a single one."

He laughed, shaking his head. "Now that sounds like your aunt."

"Doesn't it?"

"So, where did you come up with this beautiful shirt on such short notice?"

"Don't tell anyone, but I raided my uncle's closet, with Aunt Claudia's permission. There all his shirts hung, neatly pressed and smelling fresh, and I discovered this beautiful *MacWestern Outfitters* shirt. My aunt was more than glad to let me have it. She said it's too feminine for her husband. Yay me! She said he wore it exactly once. The story goes that he bought it on a buying spree when left to his own devices. So, well, you know my aunt. I'm sure she let him know what she thought about this shirt!"

"Yep. I know your aunt. She's a good woman, and I've always liked her. But ... she's really hard to make laugh."

That made me laugh! "Oh, so true, Myles. That's one of the things I say to myself about her. She's really hard to get a laugh out of. Sometimes I poke hard to try to make her laugh, but to no avail. It's a win if I can succeed in making her mouth crack a droll little smile."

The music started up again, and as it did, Myles leaned close to my ear and whispered, "I am *so sorry*, Joy, for how I treated you ... I...."

I interrupted him. "It's all right, Myles. Water long gone under the bridge of time. Everything is good for us both now, is it not?" The moment the question escaped my lips, I wanted to call it back. But too late.

"Good? Not exactly. That is, unless being in pain is good, then I'm great! The best part of my life is my daughter. I adore her and I'm profoundly grateful that she's in my life. She's so interesting, and *so different* from her mother."

"I'm guessing she's more like her father. But, OMG, does she...."

"I *know*, she looks uncannily like her mother."

"Yeah. A clone. Knocked me for a loop when you walked up with her. She's a stunner, and she's only about eleven years old, right?"

Myles stuttered, "Ahm ... she just turned twelve."

"Oh," I said, refusing to do the math on the spot. I'm the one who said it's water under the bridge of time. But if his daughter was twelve years old, then ... well, again, I refused to do the math here and now. I'm having fun dancing with him tonight. I remained determined to be in the moment.

But I couldn't help replaying a night so long ago, sitting on the bleachers in high school next to Sharon as we watched a basketball game, and seeing the way she looked at "my Myles." I had an extremely uncomfortable feeling, which, as it turned out, had been right on target.

But in this moment, Myles held me close, our bodies moved to a slow version of the old classic, *Cripple Creek*. I tried, I really did, to keep some space between us, but it was not to be. I resigned myself, with a secret grin. I glanced over into the shadows and saw Myles' daughter looking at us attentively, with a small frown on her beautiful features.

Well, dear girl, I thought, I have no intention of running off with your dad! He's all yours. But I couldn't help feeling sad for her if the few moments Myles and I spent together caused her pain. The next time we came around to where she stood, I pulled out of the driver's lane onto the shoulder.

"Here's your dad back!" I said, grinning. "Thanks for letting me borrow him for a couple of dances."

"Don't stop now! I haven't seen him so happy in, … well, too long."

Oh! I thought, her facial expression did not reveal her actual feelings—interesting! "We need a break, anyway. Or *I* do. You probably hear this all the time, but you are the.…"

"*Ahhh*.…" Myles tried to interrupt me, but with hobnail boots, I marched on. "… Absolute image of your.…"

"*Don't. Even. Say. It!*" the girl warned.

Yikes! I'd stepped in a *huge* cow pie!

"Tried to warn ya." Myles shook his head.

"I am *so* sorry! Let's start again. Myles, why don't you introduce me to your daughter?"

"Oh, for goodness sake!" he blurted. "*What* is the matter with me? How is it I didn't introduce you earlier?"

"Because when you were about to, that horrible … whatever he is, came up to our group and spoiled our mood," his daughter said furiously.

"Oh, that's right," Myles nodded. "The Dudley interference. Well now, then, Joy, I would love you to meet my beautiful daughter, Blaze. And Blaze, I'd like you to meet my good friend from childhood, Joy Forest. She grew up here, but she lives in Oklumin now."

"So lovely to meet you, Blaze." I extended my hand.

She took my hand. "It's spectacular to meet you. I'll be popular with my social studies teacher next week when I tell her who I hung out with this weekend. We're reading your book, *Ethnography and Phenomenology* in class."

I raised my eyebrows in surprise. "I'm glad to hear it, but that book is kind of tough sledding. What do you think of it?"

"I think it's brilliant. My teacher, Miss Goodson, takes the time to explain your concepts. I intend to become a social scientist. I have a lot of theories about society, and I can't wait to do research. I love living in the country, and I want to do work that helps preserve it."

"Fantastic, Blaze. I'm delighted to hear it." I looked up at Myles, somewhat blown away.

"Sorry I went off on you like that," Blaze said. "But I *hate* my mother. She left us, and in the worst possible way. I shall never forgive her."

I glanced over at Myles again. He shook his head slightly, as if to say, there's no point in arguing with her.

"There are only two people I hate," she went on, "which is probably a pretty small number. One is my mother, and the other is," she nodded her head to the other end of the barn. There was no mistaking she meant Dudley, who had cornered someone, gesticulating broadly around the poor victim.

"It seems everyone shares your opinion," I observed. "But why do *you* feel so strongly about him?"

She shook her head, almost as if she couldn't speak.

"She sometimes goes by your place," Myles said, "And thus, his place. Apparently she saw him abusing that beautiful black stud."

"Yeah. He's horrible! I saw him hit the stallion with a huge stick on three different occasions.

"I first met him—well, both of them, Dudley and the black stallion—when Dudley accosted my mother and me at the feed store, like he did tonight. He was bragging about having bought the stallion. Then he invited us, well, my mother, not so much me, over to his place to see the black stallion, so we followed him to his home. What a breathtaking horse!"

I heard one of the musicians on the stage call, "Sharon! Sharon!"

I looked up at him, but couldn't quite make him out in the subdued light. Frowning, I looked over at Myles.

"He means you, Blaze."

"Then he can call me by my name. He knows it."

"*Blaze!*" the musician called. "Sorry! Don't be mad! Please come and sing."

She nodded and stepped up on the stage.

"What?" I asked, puzzled.

"Sharon insisted on naming our daughter, 'Sharon.' I wasn't for it, but I didn't get to have a vote. When all hell broke loose after her mother left, my daughter soon insisted, *insisted*, that I change her name legally to Blaze. And so I did. I didn't argue with her, pro or con, but I was in favor of her name change to whatever she wanted."

An incredible voice filled up the barn. I looked up at the stage, and sure enough, there stood Blaze, with microphone in hand, belting out a song with one of the most powerful and beautiful voices I'd ever heard.

"*Wow!*" I whispered. "*Amazing!*"

"Isn't she?"

All the chatting in the barn stopped, all the dancers stopped. Everyone turned to look at the stage, giving Blaze their undivided attention. Did she even know her talent? I wondered.

Rushing Waters

I was walking in a dry land
The trees were far and few
Then I came upon the rushing river
And I knew soon I'd be with you

Washougal River,
Home of love and birdsongs
Washougal River,
Where my heart belongs

Oh! I had traveled far too far
Loneliness cuts like a knife
I see rushing waters, heart's baptism!
Returning to the best of life

Washougal River,
Home of love and birdsongs
Washougal River,
Where my heart belongs
Where my heart belongs....

Did she sing that beautiful song for me, about my beloved river where I live? As the song faded, the barn erupted in applause and cheers. But I could only stand deeply touched and filled with awe.

At that moment, my wrist comp twitched. *"Please, oh please!"* I begged fate, *"No disasters now!!"*

Chapter 13

Just One More Song

My wrist comp projected a small image of
Robbie. How could I have forgotten him? I
sent him a holo of Blaze on the stage, and
then turned in a circle, showing him Uncle Eben,
engaged in his chess game, the people clapping and
cheering, looking up at Blaze, the long table of food,
which now appeared rather like a battle had taken
place on it, and back around to Myles standing by
me.

A question mark floated up, and I knew Robbie
meant Myles. Well, he'd have to wait. I waved to
him and shut off the holo feed.

"Holo?" Myles asked.

"Yes. To my robot cat. I promised him earlier today I'd send one, and I somehow forgot. He called to remind me. Great timing on his part, though, to get to hear Blaze sing."

"Your robot cat," Myles said.

"Yes. And, frankly, sort of my best friend."

He looked at me quizzically. I couldn't quite read his look, but before we could go into it further, the band took a break and Blaze came back down from the stage, joined by two of the musicians.

"Hey, Joy, great to see you!" one of the musicians said. "You're looking fantastic!"

I took a closer look at him, a big burly, muscular two-hundred-and-fifty pound man. "Clint!" I exclaimed, finally recognizing him. "How did you get so big?" Little Clinton had been the grade school "runt."

He laughed. "Music and working out. Got tired of being called runt!" He gave me a big bear hug.

"Your method works, definitely not a runt now! But even more importantly, thank you for the wonderful music—such talent! I don't know when I've had so much fun."

"Awww, Joy, I'm glad to hear it. Do you remember my little brother? He's four years younger than me, so you may not know him." Clint reached back and pulled his brother into our circle.

"Joy, this is my brother, Tom. Tom, I'd like you to meet my grade school pal...."

"Yes, Dr. Forest, it's fantastic to see you. You may not remember me but I...."

"Oh yes, Tom, I do remember you! You took one of my workshops that I give at the University. I didn't realize it at the time that you were from my home territory. It's great to see you." We shook hands. It had been several years since I gave the workshop he attended, and as the musicians were in shadows on the barn stage, I hadn't recognized him until he came close.

"That weekend workshop of yours inspired me tremendously. I'm working on my masters at present."

"That's magnificent," I said. "What do you plan to do professionally?"

"I ... well, I ... I'm hoping to get to work on Pacifica."

"Wow, Tom, that would be spectacular!"

"I agree, I just hope I can make it happen."

"Let's keep in touch. I'll write you a letter of recommendation when you're ready to apply for a position there, if that would be helpful."

His eyebrows raised in surprise. "That would be *hugely* helpful. My friend, James, who's on the project right now, has said he'll help me acquire a position. So a letter of recommendation from you will certainly be an advantage."

"Betty just told me that James is on Pacifica. *Sooo* impressive! I'm looking for an opportunity to go there too, for a while. At least long enough to write a few papers, and hopefully a book. Isn't it exciting!"

"Very exciting. Maybe we'll be there at the same time," Tom said with genuine enthusiasm.

"It would be helpful to have people I already know to work with when I'm there."

Frustratingly, I heard Dudley's voice approaching us. I didn't want to turn around and see if he actually intended to impinge on our little group's lovely moment. But happily, he lumbered by us.

Unhappily, he stopped to bother my uncle, still engrossed in his chess game. I couldn't make out what he was saying despite his loud voice, but I *did* hear the dismissive tone of my uncle's reply.

"It looks like your neighbor has got your uncle in his sights," Myles observed, frowning.

I nodded. "And it sounded like my uncle put him in his place." Relieved, I saw Dudley move away from Uncle Eben. "I don't know when I've *ever* heard of a person being so utterly disliked. Other than say, certain politicians."

This elicited a guffaw from the group.

"But apparently," I continued, "Dudley intends to become engaged in local politics as well."

"He won't get our vote," Clint said with an edge of venom.

"That's right," Tom agreed ardently.

"Oh my, what has he done to you two? I've been hearing horse abuse stories all evening, and I've had my fill of it all."

"Yeah, well, we'd be adding more horse abuse stories to your list." I noticed soft-spoken Tom clinched his fist.

Clint nodded. "He's such a...." He glanced down at Blaze. "... really bad person."

"Hey," Blaze said, "call him anything you want. I do! I hate him."

"It seems Blaze saw him beating that beautiful stallion with a stick, more than once," I interjected.

"Yeah," Clint nodded. "Tom and me too. We've seen the same thing."

"I wonder why my uncle hasn't seen Dudley do that? I know he would have told me."

"Probably because Dudley beats on his horses in the paddock, on the other side of his barn, and you'd not be able to see it from you place. But when you're driving by on the road in front of the barn, there he is, for anyone to see," Tom said.

"Yeah," Blaze exclaimed, "Exactly. He's mean *and* stupid!"

"Out of the mouth of babes," Clint whispered.

"So … do you think someone rescued that horse from him?" I asked.

"I certainly hope so," Tom said. "I truly, truly hope so. It seems fairly likely." He shook his head in disgust. "The alternative is grim."

"Yeah," Clint agreed. "I certainly hope someone rescued that beautiful stallion." The two brothers exchanged a glance. "Well, little brother, we better start breaking down the equipment. It's been a great gig. One of the best ever. But it looks like the party's nearly over."

I turned around, surprised to see that few people remained in the cavernous barn. Where had this beautiful evening gone? It flew away entirely too fast!

"Just one more song," I begged. When would I hear authentic live bluegrass like this again? Probably not until I returned to my childhood home, and and there happened to be a party. Rare, indeed.

"Okay, Joy, for you, one last song. What would you like to hear?"

"I don't know, you choose."

"Nope. You have to pick a song."

They put me on the spot! I love bluegrass, but I don't know it very well. However a song popped into my mind that I'd recently heard by a young and promising artist. "Do you know *Blue Sky with Evergreens*? It's kind of new, but I really like it."

"*Sure!*" Clint said enthusiastically. "We know it, we love it. Salina Bray is new on the scene, but she's an amazing songwriter." They jumped back up on the stage and picked up their instruments.

Myles turned to me. "Last dance of the evening?"

I glanced down at Blaze. "Why not have the last dance with your daughter? I will utterly enjoy sitting here on this bale of straw watching you two, while listening to this beautiful song."

Myles and Blaze both grinned at me as if I'd said something particularly brilliant. And I was right. I enjoyed the beautiful and touching sight of daughter and daddy whirling around the nearly empty barn, as the sweet cotton candy music swelled to the walls.

Bonny and Betty and Richie, with a massive number of sleepy children in tow, came over and gave me hugs, as we shared parting kindhearted wishes and promises to stay in touch. Off they shuffled into the night, while I felt a stab of pathos.

I love my life. But sometimes … sometimes when I think about the fact that a small robot is my best friend, and I see people *I* love with their lives full of other people *they* love, there's a fleeting stab of pathos.

But not enough to change. Because, well, I love my life!

I meandered over to my uncle and sat down on the bale of straw next to him. He glanced over at me, then returned his attention to the chessboard.

"And I thought you'd want to go home before I was ready!" I chuckled.

He stole a glance around the barn. "Oh, Lordly, Joy! Is the party over?"

"Very nearly." The song came to an end, soon replaced by the noises of the band breaking down their mystical devices of music.

"Dang! And I was winning!"

I nodded to Uncle Eben's chess partner. "So, Dave, did you give him a good run for his money?"

"No money involved," Dave frowned at Uncle Eben's move. "But, yeah, it's been a good contest."

"I really miss this," Uncle Eben said.

"Why don't you play chess with Dave on a regular basis? There's no reason not to."

Uncle Eben wrinkled up his face. "I don't imagine your aunt would appreciate us two old geezers taking up her living room for hours on end."

I restrained myself from saying, "It's your living room, too," and said instead, "Why not go to the library? They have those little sound-proofed rooms for people working together on projects. You could reserve one of those."

They both looked at me like I'd discovered sunlight. Then they exchanged a look with each other.

"That's a pretty nifty idea," Dave said. "What do you think, Eben?"

"I like it! But ... why didn't *we* ever think of that?"

"I guess we're not as clever as your niece."

This cracked them both up, and they cackled somewhat uncontrollably.

"*Checkmate!*" Uncle Eben said triumphantly, still cackling.

"Hey," Dave asked indignantly, "how'd you do that?"

Uncle Eben pointed to his head. "With whatever cleverness I have!"

"Good games, Eben. I had a lot of fun." Dave began putting away his beautiful stone chess set, lovingly placing each piece in its niche in a drawer under the board. Uncle Eben began doing the same with his chess pieces.

Myles and Blaze came up to us. "We're taking off. Great to see you, Eben and Joy. Always good to see you, Dave!"

I smiled at Blaze, who, for the first time all evening, looked happy.

Myles gave me a lingering hug and whispered in my ear his long-ago endearment, "Hope to see you again soon, little chickadee," as he kissed my cheek.

Chapter 14
The Party's Over

I nodded, but, overwhelmed by a flood of emotion, I could not come up with a single thing to say. So, I said nothing.

Myles and Blaze turned, and I watched as they faded into the shadows.

Uncle Eben stood. "Shall we?"

"Yes, let's." I tapped my wrist comp, waking my car. "Come to the front door of the barn." I waved to Clint and Tom on the stage. They both blew me kisses. I giggled and returned the kisses.

As we headed for the door, I suddenly realized, "Oh, no, Uncle Eben! I didn't see the Smiths all evening! Where are they? I want to thank them."

"They went to bed *hours* ago. They came by and chatted with me. They told me to say hi to you. You were engaged in a head-to-head talk with Betty at the time, and they didn't want to bother you."

"Oh, dear. I wouldn't have been bothered! Although the talk with Betty was a delight and filled with surprising relevance." I stopped to pick up Aunt Claudia's tureen, now considerably lighter. "Completely empty, not a drop left!"

"That'll warm your aunt's heart."

"Excellent. That's all I ever strive to do."

We stepped out into the starry, starry night. A beautiful, warm country evening, with the aroma of wheat and flowers commingling on the gentle breeze, wafted over us.

"What a perfect evening," I sighed, as we climbed into the waiting car.

"Very lovely," Uncle Eben agreed. "Did you manage to come up with a companion for Grifter?"

"I put feelers out. I'm sure some creature will turn up." I thought about all of the evening's input, and the one consistent thread throughout: A universal dislike for Dudley. Scratch that. A universal *hatred* for Dudley.

"What's interesting is how your neighbor is despised by everyone I talked to, without exception. It seems to me that anybody in the territory would be inclined to, not steal, but *save* that stallion from Dudley's abuse. Honestly, I don't know how he's gotten away with it to the extent that he has."

"What you say doesn't surprise me," Uncle Eben said. "As I mentioned, he's been unreasonably rude to me."

"What's his domestic situation? Is he married? Have you met his wife?"

"No, he's not married. He supposedly has a girlfriend, but I've never seen her."

"Interesting! From the conversations I had tonight, it seems to me that Bonny, Richie, John, Myles, Clint, Tom, and even Betty, could have stolen the horse, with good cause. And that's just the people I talked to. I have the feeling that anyone I talked with would leave me with the thought that they may have rescued the stallion from abuse."

Uncle Eben shook his head in dismay. "It's a terrible thing to have such a neighbor! I do wish he'd leave."

"I do too! I don't like to have to even *think* about you and Aunt Claudia living in such close proximity to someone who blatantly shows criminal behavior. Cruelty to animals in farm country, where animals are central to people's lives! I wonder why he even has horses."

"I know the answer to that. In the brief conversation I had with him, he rattled on about a movie he'd seen, how someone made a fortune breeding race horses. I guess he thought he'd come dancing in, buy a piece of property, buy a bunch of horses, and start raking in the money from them. As if they're a bunch of widgets, and not living, breathing, intelligent, emotional creatures. He has no knowledge of country life, let alone horses!"

I closed my eyes in dismay, feeling as though I could not stand even the mental image of what my uncle said. "Well, that answers *that* question. If only I could figure out who stole the horse, and where he might be, we could mount a legal investigation into Dudley's behavior, to, first of all, remove the horses from his possession, and, secondly, fine him to the extent where he decides the gold mine he thought horses would be, they are not. And then, perhaps he'll leave."

"Wouldn't that be wonderful!" Uncle Eben exclaimed, as we pulled into the driveway.

"Yes it would." As we got out of the car I grabbed Aunt Claudia's soup tureen, and we went into the house. Only one small light dimly lit the kitchen. Aunt Claudia had gone to bed hours before.

I put the soup tureen in the sink and filled it with water. Then Uncle Eben and I toddled off to our bedrooms.

"Good night, Joy. Thank you for inviting me to go with you, I had a great time."

I chuckled, "We went on *your* invitation, so thank you for letting me go with *you!*"

After changing out of Uncle Eben's beautiful shirt and taking off my beautiful red boots, I put on my night clothes, then tumbled into my little childhood bed. Although beyond exhausted, I couldn't help going over and over the information I'd gleaned. A big chunk of *something* my mind kept saying, "You're missing this! You're missing this!"

What?! What was I not pegging together? I knew it was powerful to sleep on a quandary. The subconscious mind is brilliant, and when allowed to go to work without distraction can often come up with amazing insight. And even though I knew this, I could not get myself to go to sleep.

Hmmmm ... some little piece of my brain asked, you don't suppose *Myles* has anything to do with your inability to fall asleep, do you?

Around and around I went on these three big questions: Did someone steal the stallion? Do I know that person? What to do, if anything, about Myles?

until the birds began twittering, and the sun crested the planet.

I finally fell into a fitful sleep.

I awoke to a soft tapping on my door.

"Yes?"

"Are you awake?" Aunt Claudia asked.

"Not really." I pulled myself into a sitting position in the bed. "Come in."

Aunt Claudia opened the door just enough to stand in the doorway. "I see my soup tureen in the sink with water in it. Did you pour what was left of the soup down the drain?"

"*Oh, no!* Aunt Claudia, I would do no such thing! There wasn't a drop left—it was poured down the gullets of a barn full of your hungry neighbors!"

"Well ... that's good," Aunt Claudia said brusquely. "Are you planning to stay in bed all day?"

"Not exactly planning, dear Auntie, but definitely giving it serious consideration." I grinned. "I couldn't go to sleep—I only fell asleep maybe an hour ago, as the sun came up."

"What's got you so upset?"

I hadn't thought of myself as upset as much as contemplative. But I guess my aunt was right. I *was* upset. "I'm trying to figure out who stole your nasty neighbor's beautiful black stallion. Criminitely, Aunt

Claudia, that guy is a real piece of work. I've never encountered anyone so totally and resoundingly disliked. And I mean, *hated!*"

"I've never talked to him, so, other than how inexcusably rude he'd been to your uncle, I have no opinion."

"He beats horses. I heard eyewitness reports from almost everyone I talked with."

Aunt Claudia bristled. *"Well then, he must go!"*

My aunt could be cryptic, she could be difficult to read. But when it came to animals, she had no tolerance for abuse.

"Right! I couldn't agree more. And that's what I'm working on."

"Go back to sleep, then. You need your sleep to sort things out." She stepped out of the room and closed the door.

I told myself I'd not possibly be able to get back to sleep now. But then, strangely enough, I woke up four hours later ... still sitting up in bed! I hadn't moved a muscle. I looked at the time. One p.m.! It dawned on me that it was Sunday, and when Aunt Claudia came into my bedroom, she must have been going to ask me if I would like to go to church with them.

I got up and made myself presentable, thinking I was a little bit hungry, and a lot wanting to hang out with Grifter. I went into the kitchen. No one was there. In fact, it seemed like no one was in the house! I went out to the barn, and on the way saw both Aunt Claudia and Uncle Eben in the garden, harvesting whatever was ready to be harvested. I waved to them and went into the barn. Grifter stood munching his hay. He greeted me with a warm neigh.

I loved seeing him so relaxed and contented. "Hello, boy. You've been really good! No crying today, even though you haven't seen me all morning. I'm pretty sure you'll have a companion before long after my canvassing on your behalf last night."

I picked up his curry brush and began to give him an affectionate brushing.

"What did you say to people last night?" Aunt Claudia asked behind me, startling me practically out of my skin.

"What do you mean?"

"I mean, people have been coming out of the woodwork, offering us creatures as companions for Grifter. So far there's been, two sheep, a goat, a donkey, two burros, and several geese."

"Holy guacamole, Aunt Claudia, I can't believe there are so many orphaned animals!"

"I don't think they're orphans. I think people around here are that nice that they're willing to share their livestock with your horse, who's perhaps the most weirdly, highly emotional, horse anywhere."

"I doubt that!" I argued, although I knew it was true that Grifter was a uniquely emotional creature. "But, that's awesome! You hear that, my friend? Lots of potential companions for you!"

"What's your uncle supposed to do with all those animals?" Aunt Claudia asked, an edge in her voice.

"I imagine what needs to be done is simply choose one, and thank everyone else." I paused, reflecting on the wealth of creatures offered, patting Grifter. "Or maybe two. I think the two burros might be super-good friends for Grifter."

"*Hmmmm* ..." Aunt Claudia sounded slightly disapproving, but added no further negative commentary.

"What do you think?"

"I think I'll leave it up to Eben."

She left the barn, and I returned to currying Grifter. "That's a good idea, my friend," I said to him. "But I still have hopes that you'll see your favorite horsie in the near future."

When I finished brushing Grifter, I took him for a ride, bareback. We ambled around the pasture. I mused deeply, letting Grifter drift where he pleased, munching on grass, stopping to watch the flock of geese flying overhead, honking.

"Would you like some geese for companions?" As lovely as they were, I believed Grifter would be happiest with a four-footed mammal for a friend.

After awhile I decided that I needed to put all the bits and pieces that I'd puzzled together into a mind map. I rode Grifter back into the barn, slid off him, and sat on the bale of straw. I tapped my wrist comp to bring up a new, blank 3-D holo, and began to plug in the details.

I made an image of all the people who disliked Dudley, adding to each person a number indicating the level of their frustration with him as I perceived it, which, granted, was entirely subjective. Then I placed each of them on a map of the territory where they lived.

I added to that any additional bits of information that might come into play. And that's when I saw the hole in my musings. Extremely conspicuous, once I saw it clearly in front of me.

In fact, I had the urgent realization that I'd better take action right now! I gave Grifter a hug, then hurried out of the barn. Shades of evening fell fast around me.

In the kitchen Aunt Claudia was making dinner, with Uncle Eben sitting at the table, discussing which of the wealth of generously offered animals would be the best companion for Grifter, while, at the same time, not adding too much work for Uncle Eben.

"Hi! I hate to interrupt your conversation, but I … I have to go … do something."

"Do what?" Aunt Claudia asked.

"I can't go into it right now. I know this seems strange, but I really must go right now!" I went to my room, grabbed a jacket and my backpack, and hurried out the front door, calling over my shoulder, "See you later!"

After I got in the car, I told it to head towards Myles' home. I then called up a map of the territory, and said, "Continue on to the mile, and then take a right. We're looking for a large barn that belonged to Myles' parents."

Night had fully fallen as I tried to get my bearings in the darkness. Fortunately, the car did not have my limitations, and soon we came to a gigantic barn on the right side of the road.

"Go slow … very slow."

The car slowed to a crawl as we passed the barn. At the quarter mile I said, "Turn around, turn off your lights, and creep into the barn's driveway."

The car did as I bid. There in front of the barn I saw a Space XXX Roadster.

Which I'd hoped I would not see. Only one person in this area would likely have a vehicle that cost more than a lot of people's home.

And even more terrible, I heard shouting.

Chapter 15
Saving Blaze

"Pull round to the back of the barn, slowly. We must not be heard!"

The car crept around the barn. There stood a stand of young alders. "Park among these trees."

I pulled my AR glasses from my backpack, put them on, then got out and stole around the barn, hoping to hear and even see what was going on inside.

I feared the worst.

As I came around the side of the barn, I saw a shaft of light on the ground. There! A chink in the old barn's wall that I could peer through. I leaned down to the hole in the wall. It provided but a tiny view. "Wide-angle, 120 degrees," I told the AR glasses.

Although the light was extremely dim, I made out Dudley in the augmented view. In an enraged voice he demanded, "Move away from my horse. What's the matter with you? Are you crazy?"

And then I heard a girl's voice. She was out of the range of even the wide angle view, but I knew that distinctive voice. It was Blaze. "You're a horrible person. I will never let you touch this horse again!"

"I've had it with you *and* your mother. You're both crazy!"

"I won't speak about my mother. But I am *not* crazy. And you … you're not only crazy, you're *worse* than crazy! *You're mean!* Get the hell out of my barn."

"I'm not leaving this barn without *my horse.*"

I took a step away from the barn and whispered into my wrist comp, hoping my urgent message could be heard. "Call County sheriff."

There came an immediate reply, "What's your emergency?"

"A girl is in danger. Please dispatch the sheriff to William Jacobs' barn."

The automaton clicked. "William Jacobs—deceased," came the reply.

"William Jacobs is deceased, but his barn isn't! Please dispatch...."

"Deputy dispatched." The connection broke.

"I *said sheriff*, but I'll have to take what I can get."

I knew I should attempt to contact Myles next, but I also felt I needed to get back to my little chink in the barn's wall. I slipped back to the barn and leaned down. I heard scuffling and muffled exclamations.

I dared not wait! As I ran around the barn, I said into my wrist comp, "Connect, Myles Jacobs."

"Joy," he answered, surprise in his voice.

"Can't talk! Come to your dad's barn immediately."

I broke the connection as I came to the door of the barn, open just enough to let a large man inside.

Before me, in a faint light, I saw Dudley wrestling to get a six-foot board out of Blaze's hands that she wielded in an attempt to protect herself. The black stallion stomped around in the stall behind her, the whites of his eyes showing with fear.

Dudley succeeded in wresting the board from Blaze, just as I came up behind him. He raised the board to strike her. I grabbed it from behind.

Shocked, he turned to me. "You! What are you doing here?"

"The question," I yelled as I tried to get the board out of his hands, "is what the *hell* are *you* doing here?"

He made a horrible cackling sound. "Are you stupid? I'm retrieving my stolen property. And this girl is in big, big trouble."

Dang, he was strong! I could not get the board away from him. But, then again, he could not get the board away from *me*. I looked over at Blaze, who had backed into the stall with the horse. "Are you all right?"

She nodded.

I returned my attention to not getting killed. Dudley surely weighed twice what I weigh, and he was strong. But I have ju-jitsu on my side. Well, a little bit, anyway. I'm no black belt.

Suddenly, he let go of the board, and I stumbled backwards. I threw the board aside as he lunged at me. I flung him to the ground. The look of surprise he gave me shifted to seething anger, and I braced myself for his redoubled attack.

He did not disappoint. He picked me up as if I was a rag doll and flung me into the wall, then lunged at me. As I slid down the wall, I kicked my feet up into his solar plexus.

That slowed him down a bit, although not entirely. "What is the matter with all the crazy people here?" he shouted at me. "Why are you here?"

"I'm saving a girl and a horse from your insanity," I answered. "But how did *you* know to come here?"

He grabbed me by the throat. "I've been driving by everybody's place, night after night, going in a different direction, looking for my horse. Tonight, I saw the light in this vacant barn, and finally, I was right."

I ducked out of his hold. "I put several different things together, too, and came up with the same answer."

I heard a siren approaching. "And now we'll see who's in big trouble!"

Dudley, fast upon my heels, didn't seem to realize that the siren came for him!

He threw me to the ground and grabbed my ankle. I kicked him with my other foot, when, much to my surprise, Blaze ran out of the stall, picked up the board from the ground, and whacked Dudley on the head.

He passed out like a fainting goat.

I grabbed Blaze in a giant hug. "Thank God you're all right! But Dudley's right about one thing, you're in big trouble!"

"I don't care! I'd do it again!"

I saw myself in her, and I said, "I know, Blaze, I know. I would, too."

I heard vehicles pulling up to the barn and doors slamming. The sheriff—and it *was* the sheriff, *and* a deputy—came running into the barn.

I stepped aside so they could see Dudley.

"What's going on here?" The sheriff demanded.

"Hi, Mason!"

"Joy?"

"Yep. It's me."

"I didn't know you were in town."

"If you'd gone to the Smith Hootenanny last night, you would! What's going on here is Myles' brave daughter has gone to great lengths to save this gorgeous stallion from being abused by this—thug."

"Who is that?" He gestured to the comatose figure in the dim barn light, while turning on his wrist comp's brilliant light. We all blinked in blindness.

"It's Dudley Garvy," I said.

"Dudley Garvy is a thug?"

"And possibly worse."

"If this girl stole that horse, she's a horse thief," Mason said. "And in big trouble."

"Careful what you say about my daughter, Mason," Myles said, running into the barn, rushing up to Blaze and me. He grabbed Blaze from me and hugged her tight. "What are you doing here? What's going on?"

Blaze just shook her head.

Dudley groaned.

"Your brave daughter rescued Grifter's friend, and has been tending to him ever since," I said.

An immensely puzzled expression crossed Myles' features. "Blaze, what is she saying?"

She pulled away from her father and turned around, gesturing to the beautiful stallion. "One night I walked to where he lived, slipped a halter on him, walked him out of his paddock and rode him here. Where I've been taking care of him ever since.

"Every night, after you go to sleep, Dad, I walk over here and take care of the horse, and then I walk back before you wake up."

"I can't believe it," Myles whispered, sounding shocked.

"Believe it, Dad."

Dudley groaned again. Myles looked down at him. I watched as he put several twos and twos together. "You were here, Blaze. Somehow Dudley figured out you took his horse, and came to get it. And Joy ... no, I don't know how Joy figures in."

"I don't either," Blaze said. "But if she hadn't come through the door when she did...." She shuddered.

"I want to get some statements," Mason ordered. He gestured to Dudley. "Take him down to the station," he told his deputy.

The deputy did as he was bid, hauling off the semi-conscious Dudley, who stumbled through the barn.

"All right now, what's the story?" Mason asked the three of us.

"I have no idea, Mason," Myles said. "A few minutes ago I got a whispered, urgent-sounding message from Joy to come here. I threw on jeans and hurried over."

"Nice pajama top though," I noted, grinning at his flannel top of moons and stars.

"Blaze bought me these PJs."

"I think it's beautiful," Blaze defended.

"Me too!" I answered, enthusiastically.

"*Never mind clothing*," Mason said, exasperated, "what I'm understanding is that this girl, here, Blaze, went out on these dark roads every night for the last … however long it's been, several nights, coming and going to her grandfather's barn, two miles away from home."

Blaze nodded.

"That about sums it up, I believe," I said.

"But what I don't get, Joy," Mason said, "I don't get how *you* knew to come here, in the middle of the night, at this critical moment."

Chapter 16

Best Friends, Reunited

"Exactly!" Myles agreed. "How is it that you're here? As grateful as I am, what are the odds that you'd be here, in the middle of the night, when my daughter and one of the most unlikable people I've ever known, both happen to be in … my father's barn! Which has not been used to house animals in *years.*"

There was a significant piece of information that I'd surmised that I did not want to tell him. If I could avoid it, I intended to. I glanced at Blaze, looking down at the straw strewn floor, with a fierce frown. She hoped I'd not share this bit of info, too.

"I ... *ahm* ... you know it's one of the things I do," I said. "I put things together in my mind that other people simply don't. I heard all of those people last night at the hootenanny say how much they dislike Dudley. Including you, Myles.

"I plugged all the information that I'd gathered into a 3-D holographic mind map. From that, I start with the most logical person to have been involved, and work my way down the list."

"What made Blaze your number one suspicion?" The sheriff asked. Myles nodded.

"I suppose one of the biggest factors is I remember how much I loved horses at Blaze's age. Not that I feel much different about them now. Anyway, even though several people were furious enough with Dudley's abuse of his animals to remove them if they had the opportunity, Blaze was my highest suspicion because she didn't say that she could have done it, or that she would have done it. But she was very clear in expressing her hatred of Dudley.

"She didn't say anything like that, whereas pretty much everyone else said they could have rescued the horse themselves, or they were sympathetic with rescuing him.

"And then I thought through what everyone would have had to do to pull off taking the horse.

First of all, everyone else lives farther away. Secondly, they all have very busy lives. Not that Blaze isn't busy, but I had a feeling that this gorgeous horse, that *my* horse adores, by the way, which is my motive for finding him—would be her highest priority."

"It appears you were right." Mason grinned at me. "Now I'm sorry I missed the party last night. I had to work, but I didn't much care about the party, other than being practically ecstatic that I wasn't called to it in a professional capacity to break up some conflict."

"No conflicts!" I affirmed. "It was one of the loveliest events I've ever been to. Aside, as we'll all agree, from the few moments when Dudley rained on our party. That's when I began to seriously ratiocinate who cared the most to actually do the horse rescuing deed."

"Ratio ...?" Blaze asked.

"Think through with lots of detail."

"Right. Ratiocinate," Mason said. "Well, whatever your process, it paid off. But, now I've got a horse on my hands." He gestured to the black beauty.

"I have a solution." I grinned.

Myles laughed. "Joy asserts and wins her heart's desire, once again."

Although that might seem to others as though it was often true, Myles, of all people, should know it was not *always* true.

*   *

The next day dawned bright and sunny, filled with a flurry of activity.

Mason helped Uncle Eben and me file a temporary foster care order for the black stallion, who had not been called by any name that anyone had ever heard. It turned out that the feed store had his registered birth name as "Sir Flagington." *Perfect!*

I immediately christened him "Flag"—appropriate when seeing his stunning mane and tail rippling as he flew, hooves thumping, across the field.

Uncle Eben and I met Myles and Blaze at Myles' father's barn after the paperwork was filed. Myles rode Flag to Grifter's pasture, while Uncle Eben, Blaze, and I went ahead and waited for Myles and Flag to arrive. I couldn't wait to see Grifter's reaction when his special friend to his pasture.

Myles soon came flying up the road on the shining black, incredible stallion. *Ohhh! Be still my heart!* Both man and beast, a breath-taking sight. Grinning,

Myles pulled in the reins as Flag thundered into the driveway.

"Wow! What a ride! He's amazing!"

"It was so beautiful to watch, Dad," Blaze said, reaching up and patting Flag on his muzzle. I watched as the horse leaned into her touch.

"Yes, beautiful," I agreed, trying to sound nonchalant. I believe I failed.

"Shall we let him in the pasture?" Myles asked.

"Sure. Let's go," Uncle Eben agreed.

We walked around the house to the pasture, and I opened the gate. Myles rode Flag into the pasture. Flag looked around at his surroundings, and whinnied. Grifter, in his stall in the barn, whinnied back, high pitched and excited. I heard him stomping around in his stall.

"We'd better let these two friends get back together." I said.

Myles dismounted and began to remove Flag's saddle, while I held his reins, then I slipped off his bridle. "There you go, boy," I patted him and headed for the barn.

In the shadowy barn, I saw Grifter moving back and forth in his stall, his nostrils flared, his body quivering.

"Oh, boy, Grifter, are you excited? Do you hear your friend? Let's go say hi!" I opened his stall door and led him out of the barn by his halter into the paddock where Myles, Blaze, Uncle Eben and, most importantly, Flag, all stood watching for us.

At the sight of Flag, Grifter whinnied excitedly. I let go of his halter, and the two horses flew to meet one another.

It was a sight that … well, only seeing it can truly explain it. They wrapped their necks around one another and whinnied softly, telling each other the secrets that only horses know.

I'm not ashamed to admit that tears sprung to my eyes. My beloved horsie had his friend. And Flag was equally happy to be with Grifter. Then Flag turned and started to fly around the paddock. Grifter followed fast upon his heels, although no match for Flag's race horse abilities, and he lagged behind. I was a bit concerned he might harm himself, trying to keep up with his buddy, but, much to our surprise, Flag slowed down until Grifter caught up to him, and the two of them ran, side by side, like a team.

"*Ohhhh!*" Blaze sighed. "I've never seen anything like it!"

"Nor I," Myles said in awe. "What a sight!"

I glanced over at Uncle Eben, who was strangely quiet. Then I saw tears coursing down his cheeks, unchecked. I went over and put my arm around him. "There's our boy, happy again!"

"Yes," he whispered, brushing at his tears. "Happy again."

Without saying a word, Aunt Claudia came out the back door and joined us.

As the five of us stood there, *all* of us tearful and smiling, delighting in the incredible sight of the two united friends, I heard a vehicle come in the drive. Soon Mason came up to us.

He stood by me, taking in the sight of Grifter and Flag. "Whoa! That's beautiful. Hoke-a-moly, Joy, you did not exaggerate. Those two are like *super-friends*."

I chuckled, "Yes, they are. They're super-friends."

We watched, mesmerized, as Grifter came running up to me, and Flag followed. We all cooed and petted them, which the horses took in with their eyes half-closed, loving the love-fest.

"I hate to interfere with this life-changing moment," Mason said. "I wanted to check on how the foster care was going. It's fortunate I came at this moment, it couldn't be more beautiful than what I just saw! But I have the problem of those three mares on the neighboring property.

"I got a report on your *former* neighbor. He's got a rap sheet into infinity, and warrants out for his arrest here and there. So he won't be returning here within the foreseeable future. If anyone has an idea who might be able to foster those three beautiful mares, I'm open to suggestion. The county will pay for their feed and bedding, but that's probably about the extent of it."

"*Dad!*" Blaze said, looking at Myles.

"Yeah, I hear you, Blaze."

Curiously, even as we spoke about them, the three beautiful mares came out into the field that adjoined our field, and ran over to the fence to welcome Flag.

Flag broke away from us and ran to the fence, with Grifter following. The five horses shared a cheerful gabfest, hanging their heads over the fence and nuzzling one another.

A sweet sight!

"Well, Mason," Myles said, "I think the solution to that problem is standing right here. My daughter and I will take on the care of these beautiful creatures. But Blaze, you have to keep up with your other responsibilities."

"I will, Dad. But I hope I can come over and see Flag on occasion too."

"You're always welcome, Blaze," Uncle Eben said. He glanced over at Aunt Claudia.

She nodded. "Of course. You're welcome, anytime."

I don't know about Uncle Eben, but I just about fainted. Aunt Claudia is really softening with age, and she wears it very, very well.

"That's mighty helpful!" Mason said. "Now then, the next project is to discover documents belonging to these horses on Dudley's property. I've already retained a search warrant to search his house, and if you, Joy, and Myles could accompany me, that would be helpful, as you have a better idea of what I'm looking for than I do."

"Sure," I said. "As much as I'm reveling in this moment of the happy horses, they are busy with their own chat at present, So, let's do it!"

"Is it okay if Blaze stays here with you folks for a bit?" Myles asked Uncle Eben.

"Of course. I think we'll be fine watching the horses, am I right?"

Blaze nodded enthusiastically. "I'll be more than fine!" she exclaimed.

The three of us, Mason, Myles, and I, eschewed climbing into the sheriff's vehicle. We walked around the house, down the driveway, out onto the road, and over to Dudley's house.

As we approached the back door, I noted a low-key but extremely sophisticated security system.

Chapter 17
The Terrible Truth

"How are we going to...." I began, when Mason pulled a small device off his belt and directed it to the outdoor brain of the security system, followed by a high-pitched screech, followed by a *"ka-thunk"* at the door.

Mason pushed open the door. "Like that," he replied.

"Cool! Cutting edge technology, Mason. I'm impressed."

"It's not a complete backwash around here."

"No, it's not." I glanced at his belt and noted a few other interesting devices, a couple I recognized, and others I did not. "Some time, Mason, let's chat about your cutting edge approach to your profession," I gestured to his belt. "Impressive. And, you know, I know what I'm seeing."

He grinned. "Cool! Nobody ever understands what the devices I order can do. Not even the department. As I keep things running smoothly, they indulge me. But it'd be fun to talk with someone who knows what's going on in my bean-brain."

"Not bean brain! Not in the least. Pretty sophisticated brain, I'd say." We turned our attention to the project at hand, and stepped into Dudley's home.

Wow! Natural lighting, augmented by a system of light filters, made the entire kitchen glow with an ethereal light. There were no cupboards, but instead, flowing outcroppings of rounded and organic-looking shapes, which, I supposed, housed all the kitchen accoutrements of appliances, pots and pans and dishes, and so forth.

We moved through the house with the augmented natural light coming on in front of us as we moved. The kitchen, dining area, and living area were all open spaces adjoining one another, with the same flow of outcropping shapes which leant themselves to sitting, lying, and, probably, storage.

Fascinating—but it did not make our task easier. We moved toward the back of the house and came to three bedrooms. The first two appeared to be guest rooms. Pale grey color scheme, spartan in appearance, with the out-cropping organic surfaces, one surface large enough to be used as a bed, and the others for their various purposes.

Mason went into the closet and looked around. Nothing. He pulled a device off his belt and waved it around. It didn't seem to do anything. But then, I didn't know what exactly he was looking for.

We came out of the closet. "Weird," Mason said. "All these shapes. I love my gadgets, but I also love an old-fashioned bed."

"Me too," Myles affirmed fervently. "This place," he swept his arm, taking in the entire room, "kinda gives me the creeps."

I didn't say anything. Although I agreed it was weirdly different, I also found it intriguing. Would I want to live in a place like this? Probably not. But I'd like to try it for a bit.

We moved to the second bedroom, a clone of the first one. Same everything—same layout, same pale grey. We filed into the large closet. Mason waved his device again. But this time, a rhythmic thumping issuing from it. The thumping augmented or decreased as Mason moved around in the gigantic closet.

He honed in on a section of the wall that appeared entirely seamless. But, as he held his device near the wall, suddenly a drawer flew out from it.

"*Oh!*" Myles and I exclaimed, both jumping back.

"Another clever device," I observed.

Mason took a metal box out of the drawer, and readily opened it.

"Not even locked!" I exclaimed.

"No. Not with the security of the seamless appearing wall. Unless you have this particular toy." Mason returned his "toy" to his belt and thumbed through piles of deeds and formal papers of every sort in the box.

"Treasure trove," I whispered.

"Looks like it," Mason agreed. "I'm glad I have you two as witnesses." He took the box into the bedroom and placed it on a surface, then pulled out the paper documents, when he came upon a NFT digital legal blockchain ledger—I have one myself—where one kept the most valuable of one's possessions. In my case, irreplaceable, original work.

Mason handed me the blockchain device. "Do you know how to access this?"

"If it's like mine, I do." I saw it was *exactly* like mine, and I soon projected its documents. "*Great vegan gravy!*" I exclaimed. "He's got properties all over the world. And he chooses to live here."

"Live quietly and amass an illegal fortune," Mason said. "A house of cards that is now tumbling."

"Oh! Look here," I pulled forward one of the documents—the ownership papers for one "Sir Flagington."

"Excellent, Joy. Let me send this to my office file." He sent the document on electronic wings to its destination.

Myles, who had continued to thumb through the box, declared, "And here are the mares' ownership paperwork." He glanced at it. "It looks like they're cousins, from the same race horse breeding stock."

"Good work!" Mason exclaimed. "All right, the horse situation is resolved. Living creatures first. And it looks like there is enough documentation here to put Dudley away for a while. Let's check out what I assume is the master bedroom. I'd like to get some information about this supposed girl friend he had. So far, no information, anywhere. No pictures, no name. Curious."

We entered the third, massively huge room, bigger than the living room and dining room together. We all gasped. A golden light poured down from the entire ceiling upon the dark grey outcroppings. In the center of the room lay a surface covered in pillows and blankets, glowing golden in the light that poured down on them.

"What a sight!" I whispered. My gaze shifted to the walls where I saw animated, three-dimensional graphics of scenes of the world's major cities. "Okay, I don't like the guy, but this room is amazing. It's a museum."

"That's a good way to put it," Mason agreed.

"He's still a creep," Myles said.

"No argument, Myles." Something caught my attention across the room, and I wandered over to a lavender outcropping. Why was it different from everything else in the room? Different, in fact, from everything else in the *house?* As I approached it, a holographic mirror materialized, where it appeared as though I could walk through myself.

A curious sensation.

I looked down at the bottom of the mirror, at my waist height, and saw a message hologram sitting in the corner.

Mason joined me and pointed his device at it. It popped open in front of our eyes. If there was any way I could change that moment, I would in a heartbeat.

"I cannot stay with you any longer," the note began. "I'm not the most moral person alive by any means, but I have no intention of becoming a criminal, nor of living with one.

"I've given up my previous life with no ability to return. Not only will I not be accepted back, but I really need to escape this boring village. Please do not attempt to find me. It was fun, sort of, while it lasted.

"Sharon"

Myles stepped back with a small groan. Oh, what I would have done to not have him learn this piece of information that I had figured out, and had hoped to keep to myself. Just as Blaze had hoped her father would never encounter this harsh reality.

"Oh, Myles, I … I … I'm so sorry!"

Mason looked from me to Myles, and knew immediately who this particular Sharon was. "Sorry, Myles, sorry. What an awful way to learn an awful thing."

Myles shook his head. "No, not awful. A good way. Better than walking in on … anyway, everything suddenly clicks together." He turned and walked out of the room. And walked through the house. And walked out the back door.

I glanced at Mason. "I.…" I gestured to the door.

"Of course, Joy. Go!"

I hurried through the house and out the back door, expecting to find Myles hurrying away from here, and I wouldn't blame him. But he stood in the yard, looking across to the pasture. We could see Grifter and Flag still talking to the three mares.

"Does this change your mind about caring for the mares?"

"Yeah. In the sense of redoubling my determination to be sure they're properly cared for, yes." He refused to look at me.

"I would have done anything to not have you see that. You didn't have to know."

"What I don't understand, and would *like* to know, is how *you* knew. You were not the least bit surprised. *You knew!*" He sounded angry.

"Are you ... angry with me?" I asked, shocked.

"I guess I am. Yes. I guess I am. You knew, and you didn't tell me."

"I didn't 'know' it, but I reasoned it as a probability from the information I'd gathered."

"What, Joy, what information?"

"When Dudley leered at me the way he did at the Smith's party, and when Blaze said that she and her mother had come here to see Flag after they'd encountered Dudley in the feed store, and the look Blaze had on her face when she told of that incident ... well ... this was the conclusion I came to. I saw that Sharon was apparently stupid enough to give up a beautiful family and a life that probably several billion people on the planet would give anything to have."

Myles turned to me, shaking his head. "I apologize, Joy. Of course I'm not mad at you. I'm not mad at you one tiny, little bit. I'm angry with myself. *What an idiot!* I didn't see this, right under my nose? And my poor daughter had to bear it all alone. How could I be so asleep, leaving my poor girl all alone with this distressing information? Unforgivable."

I grabbed him by the arms and shook him. "Myles, you will not speak about my friend in this manner. You're not an idiot! You've been taking care of everything, while dealing with this terrible pain. Blaze is all right, and she'll be better, now that the two of you can talk it over. Everything will be all right, dear friend. Everything will be all right."

Mason stepped out of the house and locked the back door, glancing at our strange stance of me shaking Myles. "Uh, gotta get back to the office with all this info."

I moved away from Myles.

"Can you take care of the transport of the mares without further assistance from me?" Mason asked Myles.

"Of course."

"Great. Let me know when it's done, and I'll come by and witness and document it."

"I will do that."

Mason turned and hurried up the road to his vehicle.

Myles and I looked at each other, then he sighed. "I'd better get at the project transporting these beautiful horses. I sort of hate to break up their reunion...." We both turned to look at the happy horses.

"It's a beautiful sight. But they'll see each other across the road. And maybe Blaze can ride Flag over to run around with them on occasion."

"Good idea," Myles said, not quite listening to me.

I understood. He had a mountainous bunch of information to sort through. We walked back to my childhood home in silence. There was too much to say to start any conversation.

So we said nothing.

Chapter 18

Parting is Such Sweet Sadness

A unt Claudia met us at the back door. "What's the upshot? Mason didn't even bother to stop in. He practically ran to his car, jumped in and laid tracks in our driveway."

"Claudia!" Uncle Eben said, "he did no such thing! He's got a job to do, and he's doing it."

"He could have stopped in!"

"He had quite a bounty of documentation that needs to be, well, documented," I said. "Don't take it personally that he scurried off. Your neighbor has been an exceedingly colorful criminal character! However, he'll be on extended vacation at the invitation of the county, and probably the state, and maybe even the country, for the foreseeable future."

"Meaning?" Aunt Claudia asked.

"He appears to be a fairly big-time criminal. The good news for us is you'll probably soon have new neighbors. Hopefully nice neighbors."

"Good luck trying to find the people who will want to live in *that* weird place," Myles said.

"I'm sure someone will be found," I said, thinking, oh boy, a lot of city people would be chomping at the bit to live in that house, out of the city, away from the madness, but with a plethora of cutting-edge conveniences.

Myles looked at Blaze. "Are you ready to bring home some beautiful mares?"

"More than ready," she piped up.

I spent the balance of the day helping Myles and Blaze move the horses to Myles' barn, and introducing them to the resident horses.

"Look, Dad," Blaze said as Myles' horse, Amber, and the apparent alpha mare of the three new girls, touched noses.

"Fantastic! They're going to get along … that's a relief." Myles smiled.

"A huge relief," I agreed, returning his smile. My wrist comp jangled. "Hi, Robbie. Everything okay?"

"Everything, except you're not here."

"You're right. That's because I'm here." I projected his holo so he could see my friends and the horses, and Blaze and Myles could see him. "Robbie, these are my friends, Blaze and Myles. And those are the horses that they're going to love and care for, lucky horses.

"Blaze and Myles, this is Robbie, my amazing android cat, who guards my home and takes care of my bio cat. How's Dickens?"

"Dickens is fine."

"Good! Robbie is my all around organizer and super-friend. Sort of like Flag is to Grifter, only, a bit different."

"Wow!" Blaze exclaimed. "It's fantastic to meet you, Robbie. I'd love to see you in person ... or in ... ahm, well, in person, sometime."

"I tried to get Joy to bring me, but she refused."

"That's right. I had things to do here, which have come off successfully. And you have your responsibilities there."

"I do, it's true." Robbie agreed. "I have my responsibilities here. But, Joy, when are you coming home?"

"Probably tomorrow, Robbie."

It surprised me when both Blaze and Myles moaned sadly.

"Oh! They'll miss you!" Robbie exclaimed.

"I guess they will." I grabbed them in a group hug. "I'll miss you too! You'll have to come and visit me!"

"I love that idea," Robbie said.

"But it's more important that *they* love that idea, Robbie," I laughed.

"We love that idea, don't we, Dad?" Blaze said, looking up at Myles.

"I ... it sounds lovely," he said tactfully. We had a lot of water under the bridge that Blaze and Robbie only had an inkling about.

"Okay, Robbie. Take care of things, I'll see you soon." I disconnected his holo. "I'm hungry. Let me treat you two to dinner."

"No way!" Myles insisted. "You're our guest. We'll cook you a mean dinner."

And they did! From a giant salad, to pumpkin soup like I've never tasted, so delicious, to a mush-room soufflé that any chef would be proud of, to a heaping dish of fresh-from-the–garden giant straw-berries. Oh, Yum. A meal I'll always remember!

For all the heavyweight bits of information floating around us, we chatted lightheartedly about trivia. The happiest part of the evening for me was the privilege of sitting like a little mouse in the corner and observing the sweet relationship between my lifelong friend and his beautiful and brave daughter.

*   *

I didn't get back home until late, having told my aunt not to look for me before she saw the whites of my eyes. I went out to the barn, where I found Grifter in his stall, and Flag in the next stall. Flag whinnied at me as I came in the barn, although Grifter was sound asleep. He woke at the sound of Flag's whinny, and came over to his stall door. I went in and sat on the bale of straw. He lowered his head so I could scratch between his ears.

"Are you happy now, my friend? No more pathetic noise making, all right? I'm leaving tomorrow, but you won't even notice, with Flag here."

An intense sadness overcame me. *Goodness!* It was going to be hard to leave. This was the first time in my life that I was not counting the hours until I could politely leave. It had been a life-changing few days.

"But I'll miss you, my pal, until I can get away again. *Augh! Herkimer's angels!* I'm going back to a big pile of muddle with my project completely ignored for these several days. If I don't watch out, I'm going to have to fire me."

I chatted on with a bunch of nonsense for a while longer, and then finally stood to go inside. I needed to get a few hours sleep before I hit the road. I went around and patted Flag, and, finally, went inside.

* *

A few hours later, I put my things in the car before my aunt and uncle woke up. Then I went back inside to wait for them to get up to say good-bye. But I found Aunt Claudia in the kitchen, making a breakfast for me.

"You don't have to do that, Aunt Claudia."

"No. I don't have to. I want to."

"What did you do with my aunt?" I dared to tease.

"That's not funny, Joy." She brought me a teacup and a pot of steaming Earl Grey tea.

"Thank you. This is lovely."

She stood over me.

"What?" I asked.

"What about Myles?" she asked.

It stunned me that she would say such a thing out loud.

"What about Myles?"

"What are your plans?"

"What are my plans ... regarding Myles?" I asked, bemused.

"Yes. Regarding Myles."

"No plans. He lives here. I live in Oklumin."

"That sort of thing never stops anybody."

"What are you trying to say, Aunt Claudia? Please, just say it."

"He broke your heart before. You don't need him to do it again."

"Oh! Aunt Claudia, so sweet of you! I didn't realize you even knew, let alone cared."

"I wasn't a dummy then, and I'm not a dummy now. I *did* know, and I *do* know."

I got up and hugged her, whether she liked it or not. "Regardless of whatever my friendship with Myles may have been, or may become, thank you!

"Just so you know, I have no plans regarding Myles. Yes, he's attractive, yes, he's sweet, and he has a corner of my heart from my childhood. But at present, we're simply lifelong friends."

Aunt Claudia nodded, then retrieved her amazing, gluten-free, homemade-from-scratch, waffles from the waffle iron and brought them to me, along with her beyond-compare homemade strawberry syrup.

I've been treated to the culinary wonders of country living that would stay in my memory forevermore! You cannot get food like this in the city.

Uncle Eben came out of the bedroom and joined me at the breakfast table.

I had the feeling that Aunt Claudia told him to stay in their room while she had "a little talk" with me.

I could be wrong. But I don't think so.

I had a lot to think about on the way home!

I finished my beautiful breakfast while we talked about details of Flag's care and Grifter's happiness. I was filled with sweet sadness. After I finished my breakfast, the two of them walked me to my car. I gave them big hugs, climbed in with the gigantic care package of canned goodies and other goodies to be revealed when I got home that Uncle Eben stowed in my car. I waved to them as I said to the car, "Home, James!"

"And so now I'm James, am I?" the car asked.

I chuckled, but said nothing.

At the end of the driveway, much to my surprise, there sat Myles in his truck.

Chapter 19

No Place Like Home

I pulled up, Myles got out of his truck, and climbed in beside me.

"Now, Joy, I don't expect you to make any response to what I'm about to say. But, I've got to say it. Number one, I know when you get home you'll do the math. I did you wrong, but not that wrong. Blaze was premature.

"You went to college, and, I'm not blaming you, you were busy, of course ... but ... you didn't to write me or talk to me, or text me, or holo me, well I didn't have a holo then, but anyway I didn't hear from you for three months. I know at this point in our lives that is a small amount of time. But for me, back then, it felt like an eternity.

"And, well, Sharon had been trying to … I have to call it what it was … seduce me, since.…"

"Since high school," I interjected. "Since we were juniors in high school. I know. You may recall, I was there. But thank you for telling me this. It takes courage to bring that up. And I apologize that you didn't hear from me during those first few weeks I was in college. I can't believe it was three months! I remember being caught up in trying to fit into my new life."

I realized that I'd be grateful that he clarified the time-frame of Blaze's appearance. Whatever else may be, Myles knew me. And, yes, I would have gone around and around on it once I got home. Because that's just the way my mind works.

"Okay, yes, since high school. I let her convince me you were gone and would never return, and that she was here, and would never leave. Well, now, she was wrong on both counts.

"So … I'm screwing up my courage yet more to ask you, would you consider a life with me, wherever that might be? Whenever that might be?"

The look he gave me broke my heart. But this was not the moment to contemplate this … this … well, *this*.

And so I said, "Myles, you have much to process. And you have many responsibilities, as well. You have Blaze, who needs you completely right now. Don't be distracted. Attend to your life at this moment. You don't know what your near future may hold.

"What if Sharon comes back? She may grow up and become responsible, mature, and loving. She may work to repair the damage to your relationship. She may realize the precious gift of her beautiful family."

Myles laughed a wooden laugh. "Oh, Joy, you must be kidding! First of all, Sharon will never be that person. I've always known her to be a completely self-involved person. For some reason, I was okay with that. Even though she's unbelievably self-involved, she has wit, and she has a certain charm when she's not acting crazy, or demanding. She could be fun to be with.

"But! She was profoundly high maintenance. And I'm not ever going to be involved with *anyone* like that again. You have to know Joy, if she came crawling to me across broken glass, I would not take her back. I would have her in my daughter's life, if my daughter wants that. Which, as you see, at present is not the case. She knew about her mother's infidelity when I didn't, and I honestly think that she feels more cuckolded than I ever will, if such a thing can be said about the situation."

Myles looked at me with those blue eyes that have knocked me for a loop since I was nine years old, and yes, I would always love him. Why not? Life is a series of ever accruing events. It was not in me to try to eradicate any of these events, but to build upon them.

Myles reached over and kissed my cheek. "Car," he commanded, "drive carefully! Take good care of my Joy."

It astounded me when the car replied, "I will take care of Joy as if she's a delicate, valuable work of art, Myles. You can trust me, childhood friend of my cherished owner."

Oh, my! Words failed me.

Myles got out of the car, closed the door, got into his truck, and, without even glancing at me, drove away.

I took several deep breaths and then said, "Thank you for that, dear car, I had no idea you had feelings for me. Or more to the point, I didn't know you had emotions at all. Except on occasion in really bad traffic."

The car chuckled. "Bad traffic does get on my nerves. I don't have nerves, but bad traffic gets on them. Home?"

"Home."

I surprised myself by falling deep asleep on the way home. Both Robbie and the car had to wake me when the car pulled into the driveway. I got my backpack and goodies out of the car. "Go into the garage and go to sleep," I told the car. I then went into the house.

"It's so good to see you!" Robbie said, jumping up and down. "Can I take your backpack? Can I do anything for you?"

"No Robbie, I'm fine. I'm just completely wiped out. I accomplished what I set out to accomplish, which was to make Grifter happy. He's now elated. Uncle Eben is happy because he loves creatures, and Aunt Claudia is happy because Grifter will no longer make that horrible noise."

"And you, Joy?"

"What about me?" We'd stepped into my bedroom. I put my backpack on the bed, plopped down and grabbed up Dickens, asleep in his usual place. He looked up at me like, "Oh, it's you!" And closed his eyes again.

Robbie projected life-sized 3-D images of Myles and Travis in the room.

"What about your happiness?"

I looked at the two lovely men, feeling fortunate to have them in my life. "Well, Robbie, one of them is, ahm, unavailable, and the other has several tons of baggage.

"But I've got you, Robbie, and I've got Dickens. And … I'm happy!"

The End

Don't miss the next book in the *Joy Forest Mystery Series*!

Here's the first two chapters of *A Clowder of Cats,* which you can find out more about at:

https://shop.BlytheAyne.com

A Clowder of Cats

Blythe Ayne

Chapter 1
Security Breach!

I was triumphantly pulling up to the finish line on my project on Madagascar. There was no stopping me now! For once I'd make a deadline. My client and I would be thrilled....

The beautiful 3-D nuralnet of my project dimmed as Computer softly said, "someone at the front door." A small hologram of a tall, imposing woman, in layers of flowing dark green and turquoise clothing, stood at my front door. Then she paced in a strange jerky, and at the same time, graceful, motion up and back on my front porch.

"Who the H-E-double-hockey-sticks is that?!" I whined.

"It's ..." My computer began.

"I don't care who it is," I exclaimed.

"But, Dr. Forest, you just asked...."

"I know what I asked. I was being rhetorical. *Goodness!"*

Robbie, who had been curled up at my feet, neither asleep nor awake, stood and looked at the woman in the hologram. I heard him thumb through data. *"Oh! Wow! It's Evanora Montana. It's Evanora Montana!"*

"Who is Evanora Montana? And why are you so excited about her?"

"Well, me personally, not so excited. But I'm looking at her biography here and, hmmm ... she's pretty colorful."

As I continued to watch the interloper, she came up close to the security camera and made a gesture over the lock.

"Breach of security! Breach of security!" Computer augmented its voice.

"Yes!" Robbie exclaimed. *"Breach of security, breach of security!"*

"I got it! Quiet down everyone. That woman unlocked my front door. *How* did she do it?"

"As I was trying to say," Robbie followed close on my heels through the house as I ran to the front door, "she's a famous *witch*. I'm guessing she used witchcraft on your super-duper security system. And, by the way, as I am also part of your security system, it feels pretty nasty to me."

By now we'd arrived at the front door. "Hologram," I commanded, in order to see what the woman was up to before I confronted her. Also, somewhat daring her to actually open the door after her already illegal breach of my security system.

The hologram showed her standing with her hand over the security system, a look of hesitation on her features. She had the most astonishing lavender-colored eyes. But it was something else that threw me for a huge loop. She was inexplicably familiar. Although I'd never seen her in my life, I had

the distinct impression that we'd been together many times.

"*Weird!* What is she up to, Robbie?" I whispered. "What's your read of her energy?"

"She's … she needs to ask you a question. Whatever it is, it's very important to her."

"Is she … is she crazy? Is she dangerous?"

"No." Robbie hesitated. "No, I'm sure she's not. Although she's agitated, and it might seem to you she's gone a bit around the bend."

The woman put her hands on the door latch, and my alarm system again started to note a bridge of security.

"*Hush,*" I breathed.

"Do you want me to contact detective Travis?" Computer asked.

"Not right now. Let's see what she wants. Certainly she's just lost and in the wrong place. But, computer, remain on guard. If I say 'Travis,' contact Travis."

"Will do," Computer said.

I opened the door. The imposing woman was even taller than me, and that took some doing. Her flowing, dark jewel-tone garments appeared to whirl and swirl around her as she stepped through the doorway, even though I'd not invited her in. I couldn't understand why I stepped back and let her in.

She looked down at Robbie with a small frown. "Mechanical," she said with an edge of distaste, as she moved to sit on one of my facing sofas. The swirling fabrics continued to flow about her and finally the deep sea green, dark turquoise, and shades of evening purple of her clothing settled around her. Then she gestured for me to sit on the sofa across from her. In my own home!

I beg your pardon, I thought, I'll sit when I'm damn well ready!

I sat.

"Who are you, and why are you here? And even more relevant, *how* did you breach my security system?"

She waved her hand—I noticed her seemingly impossibly long fingers—as if my question could not be more irrelevant nor more off-topic. "Never mind that."

"What are you doing at my house? Are you lost? And again, how did you breach my security system?" I asked, determined to get answers.

"Please don't bother me with these petty questions." She stared at me without blinking. It was absolutely unnerving. Everything about the moment was absolutely unnerving. The intensity of the lavender of her eyes was like nothing I'd ever seen.

"Is that the natural color of your eyes? I've never seen eyes so intensely lavender in my life."

"I prefer to think of their color as violet," she replied, continuing to drill through me with her gaze. "I take lippylitherine. It changed the color of my eyes, previously a pale sort of brown."

"I've never heard of 'lippylitherine.'"

"No. And why should you? But, listen, I didn't come here to discuss my eye color. I have an urgent issue to discuss with you." She looked again at Robbie. There was no mistaking her disapproval of him.

Robbie became so uncomfortable that he moved out of the range of her view, and stole behind the sofa where I sat.

"Does it have something to do with my robot cat?" I asked, feeling protective of Robbie.

"No. Not other than my wondering why you have an artificial cat. But my reason for coming to see you is about a *real* cat."

"Robbie is very real to me, and I would thank you kindly not to make disparaging remarks about him. He's emotionally sensitive and neither of us cares to have you invade our home with your negative energy. Which again! *How* did you breach my security system?"

"Simple magic, nothing complicated. Let us get to the point, shall we?"

"Yes. Let's. If there is one." *Why* did I let this woman in my house? *Why* was I letting her sit on my sofa? What was the matter with me?

"Such noisy thoughts!" she said. "I cast a small spell on you."

"*Oh!*" Robbie exclaimed from the floor behind me. "That's why she doesn't like me! She can't cast a spell on me."

"What in the name of Jehoshaphat are you both babbling about? There's no such thing as casting spells."

"Indeed!" Evanora exclaimed. "Then how do you explain my unlocking your sophisticated security system in but a few moments?"

"I don't," I answered, feeling vexed.

"And you won't, if you refuse to acknowledge the truth. All beside the point!"

"Whatever *that* might be," I said, exasperated.

"What. That. Might. Be," Evanora-of-the-violet-eyes said, even more exasperated, "is, I need you to find my cat."

"Find your cat! I don't find cats."

"Perhaps you haven't until now, but the moment has arrived, as, even I, with all my powers, have not been able to discover where my precious little Bougie has disappeared to."

"Again, I don't...."

"I'll pay you ten thousand dollars, whether you find her or not. Although I'm certain you *will find her.*"

"Well, I'm equally certain that I will not. Because ... *I don't look for cats!* And I'm not looking for your Bougie. Cats are known to go off for days at a time, aren't they? I'm sure she'll be back soon." I had no idea what I was saying! I only wished to goodness this strange and stunning, over-bearing woman was out of my house.

Robbie jumped up on the sofa behind me and sat near my right shoulder. As I glanced over at him, I heard a peculiar sound from across the room.

Chapter Two
Multiple Personalities

R eturning my attention to Evanora Montana, It shocked me to see in the place of the large and overbearing woman, a little girl, tears pouring from those huge, luminescent, unnerving violet eyes.

Well, I'm not a monster. I crossed the room and sat beside her, patting her shoulder. Robbie jumped off of the back of the sofa and sat on her other side. She reached out her small hand and petted him.

"Oh, Joy," Robbie pled, "you must look for her Bougie cat!"

Reluctantly, I nodded. I didn't want to do it, but I couldn't *not* do it. "Are you … are you Evanora?"

Really, I couldn't make sense of what I was seeing. The little girl sat amidst the yards of gem-tone fabrics like the center of a flower.

I saw motion out of the corner of my eye and I turned my head to check out what was going on, only to see Dickens-the-bio-cat coming around the other sofa, apparently disturbed enough by all the commotion to wake up, jump down from the bed, and come across the house. I felt a puff of air, and silky blue-green fabric floated across my knees.

I looked back at the little girl, but the adult Evanora had returned to fill out the yards of fabric. A fascinating aroma of vetiver and bergamot surrounded us. I moved to the corner of the sofa and Dickens jumped into my lap, giving our guest-intruder a narrow-eyed study with a small growl.

Dickens never growls. I took this as further warning, as if the strange invader was not concerning enough without a growling cat. "Everything about you is disconcerting, and I'm vacillating between agreeing—although I don't know why!—to look for your cat, and on the other hand, telling my computer to call the...."

"Please don't," Evanora begged. "I do apologize that one of my personalities escaped. She is so distraught, as am I, over the absence of our precious Bougie. I couldn't contain her, it took a few moments.

Your bio cat took her away from her grief for a moment. And now I'm back."

"It's entirely too weird for me...."

"But, Joy..." Robbie entreated, "It's not about this very strange woman, and I agree with you on that count! I have nothing in my database that makes sense out of what she— or they—can do. How is it possible in the three dimensions? But it's not about her. It's about a cat, Bougie, a missing cat. And, if a witch cannot find her cat, the cat must be very lost. The cat must've wandered off, and maybe not know how to come home."

Evanora began to make a sort of whining sound, and for fear that she would turn into the crying little girl again, which I truly did not want to see, I shook my head, giving up the better part of wisdom, I was certain.

"All right! All right! Let's not get too emotional. I mean, we've already been there. Let's not go there again!"

I put Dickens on the sofa and stood, then paced back and forth between the two sofas. Robbie, Evanora, and Dickens watched me, their heads like metronomes. That did not help me concentrate. "Let's start with a picture. Please project a picture of the missing Bougie."

"Ahhhh, yes, all right." She made a complicated gesture in the air, and I watched as the form of a tawny cat materialized. She had distinctive markings that I couldn't quite make out, and a black necklace-like marking around her throat. That much I *could* make out. But beyond that, it was as if my mind refused to record what it saw.

"*Wow!*" Robbie exclaimed.

"What? What Robbie?"

"That's quite a cat!" he said.

Dickens stood up and growled resoundingly, while the fur rose on his back all the way to the end of his tail. I'd never seen such a reaction from him to *anything*.

"I'm looking," I said, "but I have the strangest sensation that I'm not *seeing*."

Evanora waved her hand, and the imaged faded slowly. "Not to worry, dear Joy. Not to worry. You will know Boujee when you see her. You don't need to look at a picture. You don't need to look at a picture," she repeated quietly.

I knew I was being hypnotized—I could feel myself going under. The blues and greens of her flowing garments seemed to fill the room, dreamy and watery. My ordinary consciousness slipped while I struggled to not succumb.

Robbie was saying something to me, but I couldn't make it out. Facing the three of them, I felt more out of body than in. Dickens jumped down from the sofa and scurried to the back of the house. He was not having any more of this weirdness!

Robbie got down from the sofa and stood by me, looking up at me, concern on his features.

Suddenly, a resounding command echoed through my little house, practically rattling the pictures off the walls. *"Clark County police! Open up!"*

About the Author....

Thank you for reading *A Haras of Horses*. Be sure to read all of Joy Forest's mysterious adventures, which take place in the world of the near future.

Here's a bit about me, if you're curious. I live near where Joy lives, but I'm in the present, about ten years before where Joy's story begins. Unless you're reading this ten years from now, and then, well, I'm in the past, and you're in Joy's present.

I live in the midst (and often the mist) of ten acres of forest, with domestic and wild creatures as family and companions. Here I create an ever-growing inventory of fiction and nonfiction books, short stories, illustrated kid's books, vast amounts of poetry, and the occasional article. I've also begun audio recording my books, which, having a background in performance, I find quite enjoyable.

I throw a bit of wood carving in when I need a change of pace. And I'm frequently on a ladder, cleaning my gutters. There's something spectacular about being on a ladder—the vista opens up all around, and one feels rather like a bird or a squirrel, perched on a metal branch.

After I received my Doctorate from the University of California at Irvine in the School of Social Sciences, (majoring in psychology and ethnography—surprisingly similar to Joy's scholarly background), I moved to the Pacific Northwest to write and to have a modest private psychotherapy practice in a small town not much bigger than a village.

Finally, I decided it was time to put my full focus on my writing, where, through the world-shrinking internet, I could "meet" greater numbers of people. *Where I could meet you!*

All the creatures in my forest and I are glad you "stopped by." If you enjoyed **A Haras of Horses**, perhaps you'll consider writing a review. Or maybe you'll write to me. I'd love to hear from you.

Here's my email:

Blythe@BlytheAyne.com

www.BlytheAyne.com

I hope to "see" you again!
Blythe